Battle Beneath The Dark

Battle Beneath The Dark
Kumar

This book is a work of fiction. Names, characters, places and events are products of the author's imagination and are fictitious. Any similarities to actual events, places, or people, living or dead, is coincidental.

Contents

CHERRY:

AN AWARENESS CAMP

That day was not like every other day. That day was about to change everything in my life and set off a chain of surprising and chaotic events in the future. All my friends and colleagues used to say that I led a boring life. That observation was not baseless. To the outsider, I led a far from intriguing life. I spent most of my day time immersed in work at the botanical lab. In the evenings, I looked after my nursery and spared some light-hearted time with granny at home around dinner time before calling it a night. Alongside my regular activities, I ran an organization called 'Green Future' which was associated with a few schools across the country to create awareness on plants and nature in kids. While all my contemporaries partook in pleasure trips, club parties and one-night stands, I never felt that I missed the 'spice in life' that they raved about because I was quite satisfied with the way I spent my time. But this day was about to change everything at once, elevating the excitement and curiosity in my life to the summit. It was this day that had brought me and him together.

The day was 17th of September. It was a crisp autumn morning in the beautiful Norwegian countryside of Flam. I reached the place after a 4 long hours of drive from my hometown Volda. Few associates from Green Future had already reached this village a few hours ahead of me. Green Future was there for an awareness camp on plants and nature for local village kids and school children.

Having never been to these parts before, I felt the village was so intriguing because of its breathtaking beauty. This village was situated in the Flamsdalen valley surrounded by high raised fjords. Making the place more idyllic, autumn set a colourful tone all over the valley with green, yellow and red leafed trees and bushes. The stunning landscape of this village gave me a grand welcome. With such a spectacular nature around, I felt I could not have asked for a more befitting location to hold the awareness camp on nature and plants. We were going to hold the camp on 20 hectares of farmland belonging to Daniel, the organizer of the event. Following the shared location on WhatsApp, I reached my associates in a secluded farming region of Flam village.

While few of my associates were engaged in setting the camp tents in the farm, I took part in unloading and arranging all the saplings brought from the nursery gardens to display and distribute to kids. At this time, Edward Bell's 'Alone' song kept repeating from a bluetooth loudspeaker which belonged to my dearest friend Anna. The song was so enthralling that it made everyone sluggish as they dawdled in setting up the camp. I was vexed due to their slow pace. I walked to Anna and turned off the loudspeaker. As the speaker went mute, everyone halted and stared at me.

'What the hell did you do?' Anna said furiously.

'Your song was making everyone sluggish.' I replied.

'Humm... Then give me your earphones, so that my song will not reach your ears anymore.'

I pulled earphones out of my handbag and gave it to Anna. She plugged in the earphones and continued to listen to the song. As the song was limited only to Anna's ears, silence set over the place. Everyone concentrated to set the camp and we did it on time.

Time was 10:00 am. Slowly, camp started to fill with local village kids and school children along with their parents and teachers. Few of us were engaged in explaining to kids about the plants and the rest of the associates and teachers teamed up to design a curriculum for kids on protecting nature and growing plants. While I was talking about the role of plants in nature to kids, one of my associate's cute little son desperately tried to catch an apple hanging down from a nearby tree but couldn't grab it as it was a bit high. Noticing this, I reached him and gently lifted him up. Getting to the height of that apple, he plucked it with a grin on his face. Seeing this grin on his cute face, my heart was filled with great content. Putting him down, I kneeled in front of him and kissed his soft little cheek.

As time passed by, kids from the local schools and nearby villages kept visiting the camp in batches. We felt so happy to see such a good response for our awareness camp from the locals. With doubled enthusiasm, we kept explaining the importance of plants in mother nature and distributed a sapling to each kid at the time of their exit. Spending time with kids and teaching them about the significance of plants gave me great satisfaction.

Time was 4:15 pm, school kids had already left the place and local village kids along with their parents kept visiting the camp. At around 6:30 pm, the camp turned empty with the exit of the final batch of kids. After having some delicious snacks in a relaxed mood, our Green Future team joined together for group photos and selfies. Then, we spent more than an hour in that location enjoying the beautiful nature around us and cracking jokes on each other.

Time was 8:00 pm, the sun was already set and the sky turned dark. With hundreds of saplings left behind, I and three of the camp's supporting staff were engaged in loading them into the truck. On the other hand, our team had finished packing all of the camping equipment and begun its journey to Bergen where we were supposed to hold the camp the next morning. Now, only four of us were left on site loading those plants.

After loading the plants into the truck, those staff had left for Bergen in that truck. With their exit, I reached back to the camp area to take my stuff which I kept beneath the apple tree. With my laptop bag in one hand and water bottle in another, I started walking towards my car. When I reached the car and was about to open its door, I realized that my handbag along with the car keys in it was missing. Thinking that I may have left handbag at the apple tree, I walked back to the camp area. Reaching there, I started searching around that tree but failed to find it.

Because of the handbag that went missing, my blood ran cold. I continued to search for my handbag while trying to recall where I left it. I then remembered collecting my earphones from Anna and putting them in the handbag along with my mobile an hour ago. That was my last contact with the handbag and I couldn't remember where I left it since. Under the dark night sky, I kept searching frantically all around that camp area.

'Could my handbag still be around or has someone stolen it? How can I find it? How should I reach Bergen if I failed to find it?' All these thoughts arose within me.

Battling these thoughts, I kept searching for my bag. But the dim glow of the crescent moon didn't provide enough light to find my little bag in those vast dark farms. As all my money, cards, mobile and car keys were in that missing bag, I knew I was in trouble. 'But fate had planned something strange with this nasty incident which was going to change my life completely'.

STRANGE PERSON FROM THE DARK WORLD

While looking around the farms for a sign of help, I noticed a dim orange light coming from one of the room's window of a nearby wooden house. This house was situated 25-30 meters away from the camp's location (right behind the boundary fence of the adjoining farm). I had seen that house immediately after reaching this place in the morning. But due to its dilapidated condition, I had thought it was abandoned or at least uninhabited. Now, with the light inside, I learned that there was someone in the house. Hoping that I could get some help from the people inside, I stepped towards the house.

'Excuse me!' I tentatively called for help by standing at the boundary fence of that farm.

As soon as I called for help, the light inside suddenly turned off. For a moment, I didn't understand what was going on. A curiosity arose in me along with a hint of fear. My heart started to beat rapidly. Stridulating sounds of insects in those farms made that chaotic situation even more eerie. With the same curiosity and fear, I crossed the fence bordering hesitantly and reached the house entrance which was on the north. Then, I knocked the door anxiously. But no one opened it. I knocked on the door once again. And it remained closed. To find out if there was anyone inside, I strode back to that window (from which I saw the light a while ago). On that window, I noticed a large hole in its broken glass at the top left corner. There was a wooden crate near the window. Standing on that crate allowed me to reach the elevation of the window. As I peered through that window hole, all I could see inside was complete darkness.

'Is anyone here?' I called out leerily through the hole in the broken window.

But I didn't get any response. Quite suddenly, unable to bear my weight, the wooden crate underneath gave in and I landed on the ground with a loud thud. My elbow was wounded. I also felt mild discomfort in my back. Whimpering in pain, I remained flat on the ground. Suddenly, my ears caught the sound of swiftly advancing footsteps from inside. Within seconds, the shattered window opened outwards with great force and a guy whose face was covered by his hoodie raised a hammer at me. I was terrified and screamed in horror. Hearing my scream, the guy dropped the hammer to the floor and hid beneath the window. I was completely in shock. My mind warned me to leave the place right away. Holding my wounded elbow, I got up from the ground and started running, trying to get as far away from the place as possible.

After running a few meters, I turned my head back to see whether the guy was chasing me or not. Then, I noticed something peculiar. He was neither chasing me nor was he inside the house. Instead, he was running away from me in another direction. Noticing this, I stopped running.

'Why was that guy running away from me? Had he stolen my handbag? Yes, this could be the reason for him to try to knock me with a hammer.' I guessed.

Still tense, I picked up a nearby stick from the ground and started to tail him. At the sight of me, he fled into the bushes. I reached the corner wall of the house and started to scan the bushes. The darkness did not provide me with a clear picture of what he was doing. But I spotted a car secretly parked in those bushes. It appeared to me that he was trying to run away in that car. My suspicions over him grew. Meanwhile, I was startled to see him run back towards the house. Hidden from his sight, I kept eying him from that corner while holding the stick firmly to knock him out in case he reached me. But it was not needed as he entered the house. Despite my heart beating at twice the normal speed, I held my nerve and slowly stepped towards that house entrance.

Reaching the entrance, I noticed that the door was wide open. My body was shivering from anxiety. Gathering all my courage, I slowly looked inside the open door. I saw him holding a lit cigarette lighter in his hand and searching the surroundings for something. He then found a shoulder bag lying next to the wall. I could see him kneeling with his back facing me as he started to rummage the contents of the bag.

'Was he taking a weapon from that bag to attack me?' I thought.

Immediately, I rushed inside and raised the stick to knock him out before he put me in peril. When I was just about to hit him, he suddenly turned towards me.

'Noooo.....' He shouted in a frightened tone while shielding himself from the possible blow with his hands.

The cigarette lighter had fallen down from his hand and turned dead and the room became dark. But from the dim light of the moon falling from the open window, I could vaguely see that guy sitting against the wall, frightened. However, I couldn't see his face because of the darkness. Though I raised the stick, I didn't hit him because he had surrendered by then.

'Just stay there. If you move even an inch, I will hit you.' I said furiously.

He frightfully remained glued to the wall in silence.

'Where is my handbag?' I questioned with the same fury.

'Handbag??? How... how could I know about your handbag?' He stuttered.

'I know you stole my bag. That's why you are running away from me.'

'No. I don't know anything about your bag.' He said, panicking.

'Then why are you running away from me?'

'Same as you, I fled in fear.'

'Don't lie. If your intention was to flee, why did you try to knock me with the hammer?' I called in anger.

'I thought there was an intruder at my place.'

'I don't believe you. I even noticed you searching for something in the shoulder bag. Is that for a weapon?'

'Weapon...! No no, I searched for my car keys in that bag to get out of here.'

I took that bag from the floor and put my hand inside to check whether he was telling the truth. What he said was true. There was no weapon inside the bag. What I could sense inside was a book, LED light pad, few pencils and brushes along with a car key. Despite some evidence that he was not lying, my suspicion on him didn't go away.

'If... if I had really stolen your bag, why would I stay here until you reach me? I should have run away even before you reached me, right?' He said shakily.

This explanation sounded logical. Immediately, I was left in a dilemma not knowing what to believe and what not to! My mind started to seek what could be the actual truth. . . .

'If he had stolen my bag, he should have run with it. Moreover, I didn't notice any bag with him while fleeing from me. Which means, he may not have stolen my bag. Was he really frightened of seeing me, which is why he ran away? But what made him so scared as to flee away from me? Did he find something weird in me???' Apart from these doubts over his bizarre actions, I was convinced that my lost bag had nothing to do with him.

I thought about where I should have been now and where I finally ended up. I was stuck in a quandary, thinking about all the shit that had happened. For a while, I didn't understand what was actually going on. It took some time for me to step out of the chaos that was going on in my mind.

A while later....

'What the hell have I done? Without having any conclusive evidence, how did I allege him?' I questioned myself in guilt.

'Oh, come on, it's not totally your mistake. It's his bizarre actions which made you suspect him. Don't feel bad about yourself.' My heart consoled me.

Anyway, it's my mistake too. Just because of suspicion, I blamed him without any evidence.

'I'm... I'm sorry.' I said to him tentatively in remorse, breaking the silence.

He then slowly got up from that wall and stood in silence.

'Do you have some cotton?' I asked in pain, holding my wounded elbow, which was bleeding.

Taking the cotton roll from the nearby table, he passed it to me. While dressing my wound, I found a wooden stool to rest upon. He still seemed reluctant to remove the hood. Because of the darkness in that house, I still couldn't get a clear picture of his face.

'I am Cherry. What's your good name?'

'Joe... Joe.' He stuttered after taking a second gap.

I completed dressing my wound and handed over the remaining cotton to Joe. Ever since I entered the house, my nose kept sensing a strong aroma which felt familiar. On a table just by my side, few bowls made themselves visible due to the glow of their radium rims. It felt that strong fragrance was coming from those bowls. So, I picked up those bowls from the table and started to sniff the aroma of each bowl. The purees in those bowls reminded me the fragrance of Summersweet flower.

'These purees were made from Summersweet flower's fragrance, right?' I asked.

He started to scratch his head, 'Maybe he was wondering how I identified the smell with the right flower'.

'Wondering how do I know about this flower's fragrance?' I asked.

'Yes...!' He nodded.

'Don't think too deeply, I'm a botanist. I even have a nursery. All plants are familiar to me.'

As I said this, he tried to ask me something, but didn't.

A moment later, I stood up from the stool and said, 'I had left my handbag somewhere in the farms and am now unable to find it. Can I have your phone to call my mobile which was in the missing bag'.

'I don't have a mobile.' He replied.

I was baffled. . . . 'How could a human survive without a mobile these days?' I wondered.

'Don't he really have a mobile, or was he lying to me?' I thought about questioning him. But I felt it was not decent to express doubts on his personal choice. So, keeping those doubts to me, I stayed silent.

A second later, I requested a light to go and search for my bag in the dark. Grabbing a lantern from the table, Joe turned on the fire and kept it in dim mode. The darkness in the room now retreated to the corners of the roof. In that dim light, I looked into Joe's face. Nearly one third of his face was covered by the hood of his sweatshirt. He had a very long beard. His hair was curly, messy and long, which held the sides of his hood. Because of that long messy hair, beard, and the hood covering his head, I wasn't able to see the exact features of his face in the dim light. His clothes appear to be in black, totally loose to his body. He was looking completely strange, like he came directly from a different planet. While I was reading his appearance, I noticed Joe glancing into my eyes repeatedly. I felt so embarrassed by his ogling and I thought, 'I should search for my bag and get rid of him as soon as possible'.

With the lantern in my hand, I turned towards the exit to search for my missing bag. Then, to my left, on the table, I saw a painting in the dim lantern's glow. That painting shows a small kid sniffing the smell of a flower while a lady at his back holding him up from the ground. I recalled the similar scene of mine with my associate's little son from the morning. Immediately a doubt arose within me, 'Did Joe observe me in the morning and paint this?'. I turned to Joe and questioned him.

'Yes. I made this painting, inspired by this morning's incident.' Joe agreed.

'Can I know why you painted this?' I asked in curiosity.

'Because, I want to recollect the similar incident with my mother.'

'Oh, that means the lady in this painting was your mom and the little boy sniffing the flower was you. Am I correct?'

'Yeah.' Joe nodded.

'Great. This painting looks really beautiful.'

There was no response from Joe for my complement.

'Is painting your profession?' I asked.

'Yes.' He replied.

Being aware of atypical appearances and bizarre actions of an artist, I thought it was pretty normal for such a talent to appear offbeat. Though keen to know more, I headed out into the farms to look for my lost bag.

With the soft glow of lantern's fire, I rigorously searched that entire farm, but couldn't locate my bag. Along with the passing time, I got more worried because I had no money left to go to Bergen.

Then Joe came to me. Understanding my problem, he offered a good sum of Krone's and said, 'You can find a bus station half a mile to the east'.

I felt so embarrassed to take the money. But I took it because I had no other option.

'Thank you. This help means a lot to me,' I said in a thankful tone.

'It's ok...' Joe responded.

'Will you return home with me?' I asked.

'That wooden house is my residence,' replied Joe.

'Oh, ok,' I said, wondering how he is living in that dilapidated house!

'I'm leaving my car here because the keys were in the lost bag. I will return the money to you when I come back to pick my car in 4-5 days.' I said.

While I was about to leave, Joe's body language clearly suggested that he was unable to ask me something. So, I asked him myself, 'Is there something you would want to say? I can feel that you are unable to ask me something...'

'I need a flowering plant. Can... can you help me in getting it?' Joe asked hesitantly.

'Sure. I have a nursery in Volda. There I can possibly help you find what you want. Can we meet in my nursery this Saturday afternoon?'

'Afternoon... No no, I can only visit there after 8:30 pm.' Joe said in unease.

'Why can't he reach me in the afternoon?' I thought.

'He may have some work during the day time.' My mind replied to my doubt.

'Ok. We can meet there at night.' I said to Joe, accepting his request.

'What's the address of your nursery?' He asked tentatively.

'www.cherry's green pets.com. You can find my nursery address on this website.'

'Sure....' Joe said.

As it was late by then, I left that place. I took a bus and reached Bergen.

Next morning, I blocked my credit cards and Sim card which were in that lost bag. We continued to have awareness camps for the following two days in Bergen and Osoyro. Throughout this time, thoughts about Joe didn't leave my mind. A curiosity developed in me due to his strange behaviour and appearance. I felt that he was a man with millions of mysteries within him.

On Saturday afternoon, I reached my hometown Volda after finishing the camps. While having lunch, I shared all the strange events with granny that had happened with Joe. Even granny was thrilled, listening to my strange incidents with Joe. Finishing lunch, I went to the nursery, which was situated next to my home, and engaged with my regular chores. As the time passed on, my curiosity rose to its peak as I was going to meet Joe soon.

Evening turned to night. Time was around 8 pm and staff in the nursery headed back to their homes. Being committed to meet Joe here, I didn't wind up the nursery even after closing time and kept waiting for him in excitement, counting each minute.

'Will he be in same bizarre appearance? Will he behave in the same awkward way like he did the other night? First of all, will he actually come here?' I was deeply immersed in these thoughts.

After spending about 40 minutes, I finally saw Joe at the entrance of my nursery. I was so thrilled with his presence. All the thoughts that had run in my mind till now suddenly disappeared upon seeing him. He was exactly the same as he was the previous night. The hood of his black sweatshirt covered one third of his face. Same long beard and black loose clothes. Nothing had changed in him from that other night, except one thing. He was now in my place instead of me being at his.

'Hello...' I said excitingly, reaching him at the entrance.

'Hi...' He whispered, nervously looking all around.

'Looking for something?' I asked.

'Nothing... nothing.' He replied with the same nervousness staring into my eyes.

'Please come in.' I invited him.

I took him into the greenhouse and turned on the lights inside. As soon as I put on the lights, Joe was startled.

'Are you ok?' I asked.

'Yeah, I'm... I'm fine.' He replied in a panic state by pulling his hood down.

'Tell me, what flowering plant do you want?'

'I want this flowering plant...' Joe said by showing a photograph which he pulled out of his pocket.

That photograph displays a kid aged 3-4 (from his back), trying to catch the flowers (which were a bit high upon the plant) in a beautiful garden. I was greatly surprised by seeing that flowering plant in the photograph.

'Sorry Joe, you cannot get this plant from my nursery. In fact, from many other nurseries as well.'

'Why???' Joe asked disappointingly.

'Because it's a critically endangered plant, called 'Diamond of kinabalu orchid'. It is found only around Mount Kinabalu in Borneo

'Malaysia'. The plant itself takes up to 20 years to mature and bloom. Once matured, flowers typically appear once every year during the spring. Because of this ultra rarity, its flowers are so expensive. Each flower can cost up to 5000 Euros in the black market, making it costlier than diamond. Thus, the plant was called Diamond of kinabalu orchid. Due to its rarity, it is extremely difficult to find this plant even in the elite nurseries across the globe.' I Explained.

I noticed clear disappointment in Joe after knowing the facts about the plant.

'Can I get this plant if I visit Mount Kinabalu?' Joe asked in a saddened tone.

'As this plant was near extinct, the exact locations of these plants at Mount Kinabalu were kept secret and protected by law. So, it is illegal to pick.'

'Then how can I get the plant?'

'These plants were propagated in very few numbers and rarely seen in cultivation. But the original plant from the wild was only available through smugglers in black market. However, it is not easy to find the plant even via these two ways. You can get it only if you are lucky enough,' I said.

It was clear that Joe was distressed to hear the answer.

'Don't worry, I will help you in every way possible to get this plant.' I assured Joe by noticing his distress.

Joe remained silent.

'Do you want to see any other plants?' I asked.

'Yeah, I need some coloured leaf plants and berry plants.'

I took him to those plants and we kept searching for the right ones. All this while, I observed unusual traits in Joe. He kept constantly looking over his shoulder and was startled even by the slightest of sounds.

After a few minutes of search, Joe selected Aglaonema red elephant plant, Purple passion plant and African Mask Plant.

'I also want a Coral berry, Raspberry and a few more coloured leaf plants.' Joe asked tentatively.

'Uh, actually those plants are out of stock for now and they should be arriving in 3-4 days.' I replied apologetically, scratching my head. 'Do you want to see any other plants?' I asked.

'No, pack these plants,' said Joe.

While I was busy packing those plants in a cardboard box, I observed Joe covertly glancing into my eyes the same way he did the other night. Unable to understand how to react to this awkward moment, I smiled at Joe reluctantly. Immediately, Joe averted his eyes from me, looking nervous. In the greenhouse's bright light, I kept looking into Joe's face while packing the plants. Strangely, I felt his features familiar. But I couldn't recall where and when we met other than in Flam village!

Meanwhile, Joe pulled out his wallet from his pocket and asked, 'How much should I pay?'.

'No need to pay. The money you gave me that night was enough to buy these plants.'

'Ok.' Joe said and kept the wallet back in his pocket.

'How can I inform you when the new stock arrives?' I asked Joe after finishing to pack those plants.

'aston.jp33245@yahoo.com. Drop a message to this mail id.'

'Sure. I will inform you as soon as the stock arrives.' I said, noting the email address in my customer information book.

'Uh... Joe, can I ask you something?' I said hesitantly.

'Yes...' Joe nodded.

'Other than that night in Flam, have we met previously? You look familiar. Even your voice sounds familiar.'

'No, we... we haven't.' Joe stammered.

Saying this, he immediately left the nursery along with those packed plants. Joe's abrupt exit after my question raised a zillion doubts in me. With those doubts running in my mind, I winded up the nursery and walked into my house. Reaching my bedroom, I fell on the bed and thought about where I met Joe previously. Was he one of my old friends? I recalled two of my teenage friends who were also artists. But neither of them seemed similar to Joe. I also recalled other old friends and people whom I met formerly, but none of them seemed alike or as weird as Joe. Still unable to find the answer, my mind kept thinking who was he and where I met him? No matter how hard I tried, I was unable to recall the exact context where we met previously. Then, my mind suggested a theory, 'Probably, your excitement over Joe was making you assume he was a familiar person'. Convinced with my mind's theory, I gave up those doubts and pulled the bed sheet to my face and slipped into slumber.

4 days later. New stock of plants had arrived at the nursery. I emailed Joe about the new stock and asked him to come and pick up those previously ordered plants. Joe replied that he would meet me in the nursery at 8:30 pm in the night.

In the late evening, my regular customers kept visiting the nursery to purchase the new stock. My staff and I were engaged in showing the new stock of plants to our customers. Time ticked to 8:30 pm and I eagerly waited for Joe to show up. Meanwhile, customers loved the stock and the sale continued till 9:30 pm. Joe still hadn't arrived to pick up his plants. Staff had left the nursery by 9:45 pm and I kept waiting for him until 11 pm. But Joe didn't show up at the nursery. His absence made my day ended in disappointment.

Next morning. It was a day off for my work in the botanical lab. So, I decided to bring my car which I left in Flam village. Picking up the spare key of my car, I started my journey to Flam by catching a bus. Because of Joe's absence the other night, I carried his plants to hand them over to Joe.

Reaching the wooden house in the farm, I noticed that the door latch was closed, but not locked. I thought Joe had gone out somewhere nearby and would come soon. So, I waited for his arrival. Meanwhile, I searched for my lost handbag in that entire farm for about an hour but failed. I was exhausted by then and had completely lost hope on finding it, believing that someone may already have stolen it. I returned to the house and sat on its entrance step and continued to wait for Joe. As time passed, Joe didn't show up at the place and I grew frustrated. I then spotted a man working in the adjoining farm. I approached that man believing I could get some information on Joe's arrival.

'Excuse me...' I called him.

'Yes...' He replied by turning at me.

'Do you know Joe, the guy who lives in that wooden house?'

'Guy!!! No no, there was no one living inside that house.' He replied, puzzled.

'But I met him here just a few days back,' I said.

'What? I have been working in this farm for the past 4 years. But I have never seen a person living in that house.'

With his answer, I felt the burst of dynamite within me. For a moment, I couldn't understand what was going on! Without even speaking any further, I rushed back to the house. Opening the door latch, I entered inside. Interior of the house was messed up with dust. There were dozens of spider webs all over the age old objects. Few of those objects were on the verge of breaking down. I was shocked at seeing the nasty condition of the interiors in daylight. As that man had said, the picture of the interiors clearly showed the lack of human existence for many years. I scanned the entire house, but failed to find any of Joe's belongings inside. With this, it was clear to me that Joe was not living there. I quickly understood that I was deceived by Joe and everything he said to me was a lie. I was utterly outraged at myself for believing him blindly. I threw those plants that I had brought with me into my car and started the journey back home.

Many questions started to emerge in my mind, 'Who is he? Where did he come from? Is there any secret world behind him? Firstly, is he a good person? How did I commit to help him without knowing anything about him!' Thinking of these, I kept driving forward in a rage.

ASTONISHMENT

After reaching home by evening, I went to the nursery. The sale continued till 8:15 pm and the day ended up with decent profits. After a while, the staff left the nursery. I sat at the counter and started entering that day's business transactions in my logbook. 5 minutes later, the picket gate on my right started to screech. I turned towards it and saw Joe coming in. My fury returned at the sight of him. I immediately rushed to Joe.

'Why did you come here now?' I raged.

'For... for my ordered plants,' replied Joe shakily, seeing my rage.

'Oh... But you said that you will collect them last night right.'

Joe stayed silent with his head down.

'There are no plants. Go and find them someplace else.'

'I'm not here to pick an argument. Please Cherry, give the plants.'

'Oh, so my suffering sounds like an argument to you.'

'Hey, listen. I tried to meet you last night. But I couldn't.' Joe said in annoyance.

'Ok. So now you are trying to trick me with another lie,' I said in irritation.

'Lie? Do you think I am lying? I waited by this place last night until 9 pm.' Joe burst out in anger.

'What?' I said in a baffle.

'Yes, I saw your plants selling till 9 pm while waiting inside my car.'

'Well, then why didn't you meet me?'

'How can I meet you with those people around? I didn't expect those people at the nursery at the time of our meeting,' replied Joe.

'What? Is this your excuse? Do you expect a business to run without any customers?' I said while wondering 'How could those people startle him?'

'I thought it was just two of us,' said Joe.

'Even after those customers exit, I waited for you in the nursery until 11 pm. In that time, were you still waiting in the car watching me?' I questioned.

'What? You... you waited for me until 11 pm?' Joe asked remorsefully.

With his question, It was clear to me that he wasn't there while I waited for him until late night.

'Yes, I waited for you. I waited for you without knowing that you are deceiving me,' I said in rage.

'Deceiving! What are you talking?' Joe said, puzzled.

'Yes, you deceived me. You deceived me without meeting me on the previous night. You deceived me by lying that the wooden house was your residence.'

'Did you... did you go to that house?' Joe asked.

'Yes. I went there to bring my car back. Because of your absence last night, I took those plants with me to hand them over to you. But there, the house remained empty without any human existence,' I said.

Joe stayed silent in remorseful state, holding his forehead.

'That house was not your residence, right?' I questioned.

'Cherry I am sorry. I never intended to trouble you.' Joe apologized.

'I don't need your excuse. Tell me, who are you? Where do you come from?'

Joe stayed silent, thinking about something.

'Answer my question, or please get lost and never show up here again,' I said in fury.

'Uh, Cherry... I... I had hidden a truth from you,' Joe said hesitantly after thinking for a while. He then said, 'I'm....I'm Joe.'

'Yes Joe, I know you are Joe,' I replied in irritation.

'Not just any Joe. I'm... I'm Joseph Edward Bell, star of the music world. So I cannot afford to be spotted by people. This is the reason for staying back in my car the previous night without reaching you,' said Joe tentatively.

'You... Edward Bell. Ha ha ha! This is the biggest joke I've ever heard.' I replied mockingly.

'You don't believe me?' said Joe.

'Stop talking rubbish. Don't try to fool me anymore.' I said in fury.

'Cherry, whether you believe it or not, what I said is absolutely true. I am Edward Bell.'

'Enough Joe, don't waste my time anymore. Please get lost from this place.'

Then, Joe looked all around and took off the top of his hoodie, exposing his entire face.

'So are you trying to convince me to believe this by showing your face? Ok listen, if you don't go from here now, I will call the police.' I said in fury, looking at his face.

Joe stayed silent, staring at me without leaving the place. I was totally vexed by then and started walking towards the counter, to call the police.

A doubt I had a few days ago about Joe being a familiar person suddenly flashed in my brain. Then, Edward Bell's image ran through my mind. Right away, I felt that Joe's face was resembling Edward Bell's face. I turned back and reached Joe, looking closely into his face. Beneath that messy hair and fully grown beard, many features in his face seemed the same as Edward Bell's face. But, instead of Edward Bell's blue eyes, Joe's eye colour looked normal. While I was thinking about this by looking into his eyes, Joe took the colour contact lens out of his eyes, revealing his magical blue eyes to which every woman had fallen in love with. Yes, he was really Edward Bell. A mighty emperor in the music world. When I finally recognized who he was, I stayed silent in a state of shock. I couldn't believe whom I was seeing in front of me. My words got stuck inside my throat with astonishment. For a second, I couldn't realize whether it was reality or dream? Staring at him, I exclaimed by covering my mouth with both hands.

'Shhh.... Cherry, please keep quite.... Control, control yourself.' Joe said in nervousness by covering his face again with the cap of his hoodie.

'How can I control myself? I came across the musical legend of this generation... How can I control myself? I had an opportunity to have some moments with that legend, which millions of people on this planet had dreamt of.' I said within me.

It took a while for me to come out from that astonishment. Instantly, a bunch of questions started to rise in me, 'What's the reason for such a handsome guy to transform into this bizarre look? Leaving Britain, was he living a secret life here in Norway? But why has he revealed his identity only to me?'. Shoving all these doubts to a side, my excitement completely dominated the moment.

'Cherry, I want to talk to you. But not here. Will you come to my place?' Joe asked.

I stayed silent, pondering, 'Should I go there alone at night.'

'I want to talk a deal with you. If you are interested, you can come with me,' said Joe in a polite way.

After thinking for a while, I agreed to visit there because of his polite request.

'Can I know where we are going?' I asked

'Oakrill, my private island,' replied Joe.

After winding up the nursery, we both started our journey to Oakrill in Joe's Volkswagen Golf. Strangely, his car was also peculiar like him. Every window of that car was black tinted and the exterior colour was painted in black. The interior was also designed in black theme same as the exterior. My assumptions on celebrities' opulent cars were questioned after seeing Joe's car which looked so simple and odd.

'What's the need for one of the world's elite to reach a small nursery like mine to buy plants? What will he do with those plants? What's his connection with painting?' I kept thinking about these while on the way to the island.

Though my mind raised these questions, my mouth remained shut without asking Joe any question because I was still in shock. Oh, how many people in this world got this opportunity to sit and travel alongside such an iconic person. Indeed, I'm the lucky one. I still can't believe whether the moment was reality or dream! As I was completely overcome by amazement, I didn't even speak a single word with Joe.

2 hours later.... Car reached a small building at the coast of the Ocean. I did not know the exact name of the place. I did not think it had a name because there was no sign of any households around. Car entered the building and moved towards the cellar. Once we reached the cellar, I was shocked at seeing so many hypercars all around. There were Bugattis, Aston Martins, Ferraris, Lamborghinis and other expensive cars which I don't even know. I didn't understand why Joe was using a simple Volkswagen Golf instead of using these expensive cars??? Though I thought about asking what the reason was for not using these cars, I felt it was none of my business and remained silent. Parking the car in the cellar, we walked to the backyard of that coast building. I was stunned at seeing the beauty of that backyard. It was situated right at the edge of Ocean and consisted of a long narrow wooden dock in the Ocean waters. There were two small yachts on either side of that dock. In the background of those yachts, under the dim glow of flickering greenish aurora borealis, my eyes caught the spectacular view of a small hill island situated in the middle of the Ocean, a small distance from the coast. There were high raised mountains surrounding the island's left and right. Those mountains were spread into the Ocean from the coast. I was completely awestruck by seeing the spectacular view to my front. Then, Joe invited me into the yacht. As I got in, Joe took the helm

and started sailing towards the island. While approaching that island, I realized its large size. It was approximately a mile in width and about 350 meters in height. The front side of that hill island was totally occupied by trees and bushes. Apart from those trees and bushes, I didn't see a single structure on the forepart of that isle.

Yacht reached a small dock which was at the centre of the island. Just a few meters from that dock, there was an elevator door. We reached it and Joe typed a password. The door opened and we entered in. When the elevator was moving up, I was surprised to know that Joe's island was just 25 miles north of Alesund, where I had been working as a botanist for the past 3 years. But strangely, no one including me had ever heard about Joe's existence here. The elevator reached to a halt. As soon as the door opened, there was a huge opulent lobby to my front. In the middle of that lobby, a large golden crystal chandelier was lit in soft yellowish light. Apart from that chandelier's glow, there was no other light in the lobby. That soft yellow light from the chandelier fell on the glossy white marble floor and reflected to the ceiling, providing just enough light to see what was around. We got out of that elevator and sat on a couch.

'Waiting in the lobby, come fast,' Joe spoke to a person by picking up a walkie-talkie from the table in front.

Without even speaking a word to Joe, I kept looking at that lobby, amazed by its grandeur. Unlike other lobbies, which consist of couches and chairs, this lobby had only one couch on which we both sat. Because of this, the entire area seemed so spacious. In the middle of the lobby, there was a tall fountain engraved with sculptures of flying birds. I was surprised for not finding a single window in the lobby to see the outside world.

A while later, I saw an electric cart coming towards us from a narrow tunnel which was a few meters behind that fountain. Seeing that tunnel, I then understood that the entire lobby was built inside the hill of that island. I was astounded by this. Cart reached us and a tall handsome guy, aged 30-35, in a casual black outfit, stepped down from it by looking at me in shock. Meanwhile, Joe stood up and I did the same.

'He is Aston. My friend and my secretary.' Joe said by introducing him to me.

'Hello, this is Cherry,' I introduced myself to Aston.

'Cherry... as per protocol, electronic devices are not allowed inside. So, can you please keep your mobile and other gadgets inside that table,' Aston said by pointing his finger towards the table that was in front of the couch.

'Sure.' I said and kept my mobile inside that table drawer.

We both took the back seat in the cart and Aston steered it from the front. Cart started moving towards the rear end of that island via tunnel, which was constructed through the hill.

'Joe or Edward Bell, how should I call you?' I asked Joe, my voice echoing inside the tunnel.

'Call me Joe, just Joe.'

'Joe... Can I ask you something?'

'Yeah,' Joe permitted.

'Few years ago, I read an article which mentioned that you born here in Oslo. Being a Brit, what's your relation with Norway?'

'Uh... I'm... I'm only half Brit. My father was British and my mom was Norwegian. She was born and brought up here in Flam village.' Joe said this in hesitation, seeming to think whether it was wise to reveal it.

I was excited to know that Joe's mother was Norwegian.

'Oh! So you are of Norwegian descent.' I said with excitement.

'Yeah...' Joe replied.

'Norway and England, both countries are too far. So how did your parents come together?'

'They met in Oxford during Post Graduation,' Joe replied uneasily probably because of my queries on his personal matters.

Though I noticed his uneasiness, my enthusiasm didn't stop me from talking further.

'Even my parents come from different cultures. My mom is Norwegian and my dad is from India.'

'I can understand that. You look more Indian than Norwegian.' Joe expressed this opinion tentatively.

'Yeah. I look like my father.' I replied with a smile. 'Uh... are your parents here?' I asked Joe after a second's gap.

'No, I'm staying here alone.... What about your family?'

'Family... What to say! Once upon a time, we were the happiest. But fate had played a nasty game with us. My mom died 11 years ago in a car accident. After her death, dad along with my brother moved to Agra which was dad's native place. I stayed back here with granny, looking after the nursery inherited from my mother,' I said.

'I'm... I'm sorry,' Joe said.

'Whenever I recall my family split, it hurts. But still, I have a very good relationship with my father and brother,' I said.

A while later, cart exited the tunnel and I saw a lavish estate to my front in the large open area of that island.

'. . . Oh my goodness! . . .' I whispered in astonishment by seeing the grandeur of that estate.

The tall hill was vertically cut down to 50 meters from the middle of the island towards the entire rear side. There was no hill above us after exiting that tunnel. What I could see over my head was the staggering beauty of the aurora sky. On the flatly trimmed surface of that hill island, there was a huge garden spreading from the middle towards the rear end. On the rear side, under the glittering aurora sky, I saw a gigantic building in British architecture with a large dome on its top. There was a huge fountain in front of that building. Just like the fountain inside that lobby, this was also engraved with flying birds. On seeing bird engravings all over, I understood that Joe had a strong emotional connection to birds. On the right corner of the island there was a golf course, and the left corner consisted of a helipad. Cart kept moving forward towards that building on the asphalt pathway. There were thin canals (of 2 feet width) on either side of the pathway. My nose captured a sweet fragrance from the floating waters of those canals. This fragrance gave rise to a pleasant mood in me.

With all this grandeur, that estate seemed like a mini empire. . . 'An empire that was hidden from the rest of the world'. . . Due to the height of the hill on the front portion of island, entire estate behind it was concealed. There was a vast open Ocean at the rear end of that estate. Left and right sides of that island were also surrounded by Ocean waters. On either side, there were high mountains a bit far from the island which were spread into the Ocean from the coast. With all these, the estate was totally concealed from all four ends. I felt this place was the perfect hideout for a top celebrity like Joe during days off.

Cart reached that building and we entered inside. Even the lobby in that building was poorly lit with dim lights. From that lobby, Joe took me into a painting gallery room. As soon as I entered that room, a few aromatic fragrances welcomed me. Initially, I could not understand where those fragrances were coming from. But while reading those paintings from up close, I realized the fragrances were coming from those paintings themselves.

'Joe... I can feel the fragrance from these paintings!' I said excitedly.

'Making paintings with smell is my signature style,' replied Joe.

'What???' I said in wonder.

'Yes Cherry, I make use of senses such as smell and sounds in my paintings according to the scene and mood of the portrayal.'

'This is unbelievable. Joe, but how do you do this?' I asked in amazement.

'Firstly, I carefully select a particular fragrance of shrub or flower to define, match, or create a mood in my painting. Then, I extract the fragrance of that flower into oil. I mix that fragrant oil with chemicals for a long lasting fragrance. I then blend this fragrant oil with the ground pigments and purees made of different coloured leaves, flowers, vegetables and fruits or any other natural substances like these which have no smell. I then paint these purees over the canvas and the fragrance is ingrained into the fibres of the canvas. Once this is done, I capture specific sounds relating to the scene in the painting. I also compose music to set a mood to that painting. With all these, my painting expresses smell and sounds provoking the mood in it. This style also portrays all the elements related to smell and sound in the scene of my painting.' Joe explained.

'Wow... I have never heard about paintings in this style. This is truly unique.' I said in astonishment.   'But Joe, fragrance on the canvas doesn't last long, right. What will you do when the smell completely evaporates?'

'Because of the chemicals used, the smell can last up to 4 months on the canvas. But after that, I need to spray the same fragrance on the painting whenever needed.'

I was mighty impressed by Joe's signature style and such spectacular art work. I understood that painting was also an important part of Joe's life alongside music.

'So, you are a musician, singer, song writer, artist and even a perfume maker. Wow, you are truly special.'

'You are praising me a lot.' Joe said uneasily.

'No no, I truly mean it.'

'Anyway, I only have a modest understanding of perfume making. I learned this because of my paintings,' said Joe.

Meanwhile, Aston brought us coffee. Taking the cups, we both walked into the adjoining painting room and sat on a couch. Inside that room, I saw the ongoing painting of a little kid chasing butterflies.

'Currently I'm working on that painting, and I need different coloured plants, fruits, flowers to prepare Colours. Being a celebrity, it is difficult for me to visit your nursery. So, can you help me by bringing the wanted plants?' Joe asked tentatively.

'I understand your concern, Joe. Being so popular is not easy. Don't worry about plants, just drop an email whenever needed and I will bring them to you.'

'Thank you.' Joe said by leaving a tiny smile on his lips.

'It's my pleasure. But Joe, you should bear the transport expenditure.' I said and sipped my coffee.

'Sure...' He accepted.

'So, is this the deal you wished to offer me?'

'Yeah. We could have set this deal at the nursery itself but I thought I here I could introduce you to my painting style. This way you can also understand the significance of plants in my paintings.

That was the reason to invite you here.' Joe said and sipped his coffee.

Finishing my coffee and signing the deal, I decided to leave. Joe and Aston accompanied me to the coast building. Aston got into the car to drop me back.

'Cherry, keep this meet secret. Please don't reveal about me to anyone, not even to your grandma' pleaded Joe, while opening the car door for me.

'Don't worry. I will keep this top secret.' I assured him. 'But Joe... Why did you reveal this only to me?'

'Because I trust you. I trusted you for your commitment to help me by taking those plants to Flam despite my absence in the nursery. Moreover, I did not want to deceive you anymore by hiding my identity.'

Overwhelmed by Joe's answer, I grinned and got into the car. Car moved forward, but my thoughts remained back with Joe. Because of the affection and respect Joe had shown towards me, I felt that he had some feelings for me. My heart suggested that this was the true reason for Joe to reveal his identity only to me. Though I felt this, I decided to stay calm until completely knowing Joe's stance towards me.

I reached home and that day remained a special one in my life. Falling on the bed, I recalled all the weird moments between us in Flam village. With those memories running through my mind, I giggled in excitement while also embarrassed for having such freaky moments with legendary person like Joe. Meeting Joe and earning his respect, I felt great pleasure. This pleasure kept me from sleeping that night.

NEW LIFE

2 days later. I got an email from Joe saying he needed some coloured leaf plants, flowers which have no smell, raw fruits and coloured soils available in the nursery. Along with Joe's mentioned plants and soil pigments, I also packed Rosa rubiginosa sapling as a gift for Joe and started my drive to the island. I had this habit of gifting a sapling to the people I knew as a sign of good relationship and also to make them contribute to nature by planting it.

After reaching the coast building, Aston took me to the island in a yacht. I entered the painting studio and saw Joe busy working on the painting.

'Hi Joe...' I greeted.

He halted and turned towards me.

'Oh, hi Cherry...' said Joe excitedly and reached me.

'Did I disturb you?'

'No no....'

'I brought all the mentioned plants.'

'Where are they?' Joe asked.

'Down, in the lobby,' I replied.

'Ok... Cherry, have you got any information about the Diamond of Kinabalu orchid?'

'I kept searching, but I still don't know where we could find that plant.' I replied in a sorry tone.

Joe became upset with my answer.

'Don't worry. I will try my best to find it.' I assured him.

But my assurance did not improve his mood.

'Come to the lobby and check the plants.' I said.

'Yeah... let's go.' Joe said.

Both of us reached the lobby and Joe started to inspect those plants. He then found Rosa rubiginosa sapling.

'What's this? I didn't mention this plant.'

'That's a small gift from me.'

'Oh... Thank you Cherry.'

'Come on Joe, don't simply thank me. Instead, I need a favour from you.'

'Favour! What should I do?'

'I need you to contribute something to nature. So please, plant this sapling?' I asked.

'That's great. I will surely do it.' Joe accepted my request.

Under the evening sun, in a small flower garden at the back end of the gigantic main building, Joe started to plant. I was amazed by the beauty of the place and kept looking all around in astonishment. That place was host to an oak tree with broad roots spreading all over. A specially designed mattress was perfectly placed upon those roots (like a bed under the tree). This tree was at the edge of island's cliff, with Ocean waters 20 meters beneath. On the right side of the tree, just beside the bed, there was a long narrow dock in the Ocean. To the front of the tree, there was a pool reflecting the main building in its waters. We both were in the garden that was just on the left side of the pool. The pleasurable music of Ocean waves hitting the island's cliff, soft chirping voices of birds and whispering wind made the scene even more idyllic. With breathtaking beauty around and pleasant music from nature, the place seemed like heaven on the earth.

'Wow... Joe, this is amazing!' I said in wonder.

'Thank you. I named this place open bedroom.' Joe said while planting.

Meanwhile, I observed Joe glancing at my eyes just as he had done previously.

'Concentrate on planting, not on me.' I said, turning my eyes from Joe.

'Your... your eyes are so beautiful.' Joe said tentatively.

'Thanks for the compliment.' I said with suppressed excitement while my heart cavorted in delight due to praise from such a great guy.

'Cherry... Dinner?' Joe asked hesitantly just after finishing planting.

I smiled, accepting his offer.

Evening turned to night. As I loved salmon, Joe's chef prepared Honey garlic salmon, Smoked salmon risotto and Shepherd's Pie for dinner. Under the light of the dining room, Joe and I started dining, sitting opposite to each other.

'Umm, yummy. Your chef simply nailed it.' I said by placing a piece of Honey garlic salmon to my mouth.

'Yeah. He's a master at preparing them.'

'Joe... why haven't you released any album for the past two years?' I asked tentatively.

'I decided to take time out for myself, and I did not want my stardom to interrupt this precious time. That's why I stayed calm far away from the world without releasing any album since two years,' Joe replied.

'That's nice. You are relaxing this time here in Norway, am I correct?'

'Uh... Yeah,' said Joe, hesitantly.

'Your break caused heartbreak to many of your fans. Do you know, my friend Anna is a great admirer of your music and likes you a lot. If I say that you are staying here in this island, she will swim the Ocean to meet you. She was that mad about you.' I said in giggle.

'Keep your friend aside for a while. Tell me about you, don't you.... don't you like me?' Joe asked tentatively.

'What?' I said jolted, dropping the fork on my plate.

'I mean.... I'm... I'm asking you about my music.' Joe said in stuttering and consumed a spoonful of Shepherd's Pie.

Though Joe tried to get away from this, I could understand his intention.

'Yeah... I love your music like every other person on this planet.' I said with a smile.

Joe smiled nervously in reply.

Time during dining had passed as we locked eyes plenty of times. Our eyes talked to each other more than our words. I clearly felt the fondness in Joe's magical blue eyes for me. I never saw such deep affection in a guy any time previously. That fondness pierced my heart.

'Oh, enough. Please don't look at me like this.' I tried to say. But I could not because his looks kept melting my heart, giving me great pleasure.

Not once in my lifetime, did I ever dream that I could spend such a lovely moment with a renowned person like Joe! As everyone says, how weird life is. One missing bag had brought two different souls from separate worlds together.

After having dinner, I decided to leave. Joe paid for the plants and accompanied me to the coast building. While sending me off, his face clearly said he was doing it with a heavy heart. His eyes kept pleading with me not to leave, but he remained silent.

'I'm not going away too far. Just inform me whenever you want. I will be here.... I mean with plants.' I said with a comforting smile, noticing distress in Joe's eyes. Saying this, I got into my car and drove from there.

As days passed by, I continued to show up in the island with different plants, fruits, vegetables and soil pigments. Using these, Joe kept working on his painting that showed a small kid chasing butterflies. Joe told me that this painting captured the happiest memory from his childhood. It was obvious to me that the little kid who was chasing butterflies in that painting was none other than Joe.

As days flew by, we continued to have some great times in the island. During our time together, Joe never showed any attitude or ego of being a super star. Moreover, he treated me with great admiration. This impressed me a lot. In no time, we became very close to each other. He could be a top celebrity to this world, but I showed no interest in his stardom anymore, just enjoying some good times with him. Because of Joe's tenderness and affection towards me, I started to fall for him.

Though many guys fell for me in the past, I never reciprocated their interest. But now, why am I falling for Joe? Well, why shouldn't I...? He was a very good guy with a soft nature. He respects me and has a special place for me in his heart. Very handsome, at least in the past, and even now if he abandoned his odd look and super wealthy. These are the qualities in a guy any woman would fall for.

One night on the island, I sat in front of a Grand Piano and started playing 'I wanna forgive you' which was one of Joe's most celebrated songs. Because I had zero knowledge on how to play Piano, I totally messed up the tune. Joe was standing by the wall as he giggled. He reached my back and leaned towards me, touching his chin on my right shoulder. His soft breath whispered in my right ear. His palms gently reached my hands on the piano and his forearms surrounded my navel. Suddenly, my heartbeat rose. I felt goosebumps all over my body. Holding my hands, Joe guided them on the piano. Immediately, the shoddy tune turned to a beautiful one, just like the original one. His soft breath kept caressing my ear and his touch made me mad. I desperately yearned to kiss Joe and let out my love for him. But since I was expecting Joe to express this first, I concealed my feelings within me intending Joe to take initiative. It's a girl's thing to expect a guy to take initiative in these matters. Joe continued the play from behind. I was so aroused and was not in control anymore. Unable to get hold of myself any longer, I got up from the piano before doing anything crazy and said to Joe that I want to leave for home.

As I didn't know how to drive the yacht, Joe came to drop me at the coast building. We reached the lobby and I walked straight into the elevator, completely forgetting that I left my mobile in the table drawer.

'Cherry... you forgot your mobile.' Joe said a bit tentatively, standing outside the elevator.

I walked to the table and picked up my mobile from it. Strangely, I saw my lost handbag placed beside that table. I picked it up and stared back at Joe.

'I found it in the bushy grass at Flam farm yesterday. I recognized this bag belongs to you with the license card inside.' Joe said.

There was no excitement at getting back my lost bag. Well, how could it be when I was totally disturbed by Joe's touch. Holding that bag, I walked into the elevator without even looking at Joe.

Joe drove the yacht to the coast building. Reaching there, I got into my car and left for home.

Reaching my room, I threw that handbag on the bed and plunged into the chair. Though I left Joe, his touch and my desire to kiss him kept disturbing me. To divert my mind, I took my laptop and started preparing botanical research notes. But I could not prepare my notes as I was distracted by thoughts of Joe. So, I shut the laptop. I took a deep sigh and plunged into the bed. With the handbag lying beside me, I picked it onto my lap and opened its zipper. Inside the bag, there were my car keys, mobile, money, cards and all my other stuff that were lost along with that bag. Strangely, I found a letter inside. Picking up that letter, I started reading it.

Letter

Cherry... It has been a long time since I found a new aspect in my life. The walls I had built around me had restricted me from finding what I wanted. There were very few individuals who came close to me by smashing them. My mom, Aston and now you. You opened a way in my life which I had never even dreamed about. Your fascinating eyes penetrated me and made me cross my obstacles to reach you. Your intimacy was the most beautiful thing that happened in my life. This world treated me like a superstar, by completely forgetting that I'm also human. But you treated me as a true human. Cherry, I wanted to tell you that other than my mom, no one has

helped me like the way you have done in such a short period of time. I strongly feel that the relation between us is not restricted to purveyor and customer. I believe there is much more between us. I tried to express this to you many times previously but couldn't. Fortunately, by finding this bag, I could convey my intention at least through this letter. Cherry, I'm in love with you. Will you be my better half? I'm not asking you this as Edward Bell. I'm asking this as an ordinary guy who wholeheartedly craves your company....
Eagerly waiting for your response.
Joe.

After reading that proposal from Joe, I was delighted. My heart craved to express its feelings for Joe as soon as possible. Holding the excitement within me, I drove all the way back to the island in a rush.

Reaching the island, I saw Joe wandering in the lobby thinking of something. Spotting me, he stood stunned. Seeing Joe in front of me, all the excitement which I held within me came bursting out at once. My eyes filled with delightful tears. My heart strongly felt that he belonged to me now. What I had not done a few hours ago, I craved to do it now. With great passion, I sprinted towards Joe and grabbed him into a hug and kissed him with deep fondness. Holding him in hug, I expressed my feelings for him, saying. . . 'I too love you baby'. . .

As days passed by, my life turned a new leaf. Joe became a major part of my life. Working in the botanical lab during day times, spending some intimate time with Joe at the island in the evenings, and getting back home in the nights became my daily routine. As I was unable to look after the nursery because of this new schedule, I assigned it to a manager to take care of it. I even lied to my granny that I was allocated to a new project in the botanical lab and should work on it until 9:00 pm. Poor granny believed me, but the reality was different.

I never missed going to the island in the evenings after my work. During these times, we used to water the plants in the island, talked about how our day had gone at work, prepared colours for painting, and engaged in other activities like having snacks and dinner. Though we had some romantic moments in these times, we hadn't fornicated.

One could wonder why I was keeping our relationship secret. It was because of Joe. Being a celebrity, he feared that revealing our relationship could ruin our privacy. Joe's concern made sense. So I kept calm hiding this truth from the world. But I was so eager to reveal our relationship at least to granny, my family in India and to my closest friends. I kept waiting for the right time to announce our relationship to them.

One night, after hectic work at the lab, I reached the island exhausted. My ongoing period had caused mild cramps and irritation. To ease this, I decided to take a small walk alongside Joe. We both started walking on the pathway situated at the edge of the island with the ocean to its left and golf course to its right. There were narrow canals of 2 feet width on either side of the pathway. Water in those canals emitted an aroma which resembled the scent of Arabian jasmine. Whispering winds and sounds of waves from the Ocean played a melodious tune in my ear. High above us, nature had painted its own emotion in the form of aurora borealis with stunning green coloured arcs combined with a tinge of pink. The Aurora Borealis kept reflecting on the flickering Ocean waters, and high raised mountains at the far distance in the Ocean glowed under the aurora spectacle. This dazzling beauty along with the melodious tune of nature and sweet smell from the canal waters, put me at ease. On the right side, there were a row of light poles at the edge of that pathway. Even these poles were carved with flying bird designs from top to bottom. On top of the light pole, I saw a bird's nest. I noticed many of these nests on top of each light pole.

'Birds birds birds.... Why do birds have such a prominent role all over the island?' I asked in curiosity while walking forward.

'Because I love seeing them fly. They have no barriers, no boundaries whatsoever. We can never fly like them with freedom and happiness, crossing all our barriers.' Joe replied, looking up at the nest.

'But you know something... I can fly like them.' I said.

'What...?' Joe said, clearly baffled as he stopped walking.

'Yes Joe, I can fly.' I said stopping too.

'But how?' Joe questioned.

'Because I'm a paraglider,' I said.

'Really....' Joe said in excitement.

'Yeah... Being a nature lover, I learned it during college days to enjoy the beauty of nature from the sky. I have even participated in paragliding competitions and won many medals.'

'Oh, that's great. You are truly a brave woman,' said Joe.

Joe's praise automatically brought a grin to my lips.

'I don't know how to fly like you. That's why I made a place to spend some time with birds and to see them flying from up close.'

'What? You mean like a bird house?' I asked curiously.

'Yeah, you guessed it right. You wanna experience it?'

'Sure....' I said in excitement.

We reached the right end of that island, the place I had never visited before. Under the staggering beauty of the greenish aurora sky, I saw a massive Oak tree situated in the lawn right at the border of the island's cliff. Wide trunk of that tree penetrated into the ground with roots spreading all around. Long branches of the tree covered the extensive area of the lawn. Some of the branches were even spread straight into the Ocean beneath. Upon a broad branch of the tree, there appeared a small house of roughly 10x10 in width at 15 feet high above us. The roof of that house was almost touching the branches above. That tree house looked exactly like a nest made up with twigs, sticks, dried grass clippings and dead leaves. 'Oh my goodness!!! Is this house made by humans or by birds themselves!' I said in astonishment.

'You have to see your stunned face now. It is truly indescribable.' Joe chuckled.

I didn't even react to Joe as I was still stunned at the house.

'Let us get in,' Joe said and walked towards that tree trunk.

We both climbed the steps from the bottom of the tree trunk to reach the tree house. I remained in astonishment, looking up at that house while climbing those steps.

As greenish aurora glow falling through the wall openings, interior of that house had just enough light to see what was around. I was so amazed at seeing the interior of that house. All the walls and even the floor seemed like it had been made from twigs, sticks and dried grass clippings. There are numerous wooden nests attached to the walls. While I was looking at the birds in those nests, Joe tapped my shoulder and I turned.

'Cherry, come let's go upstairs' Joe whispered, pointing his finger towards the attic stairs (which were situated to my left).

We climbed up to the attic. That attic roof was very short, less than a meter in height, and the roof above had touched our heads. From the right side of the attic, a soft green beam from the aurora sky was falling through the small opening of the wall. Under the beam of green light, I saw a round nest shaped bed placed on the floor of the attic. That bed was designed to look the same as a bird nest made with twigs and dried grass. I was completely thrilled at seeing this. We slowly crawled towards the bed and settled on it.

'Wow! This is truly amazing.' I said, amazed.

Though I expressed my amazement, Joe did not reply. Staring deeply into my eyes in silence, he caught the hanging rope, which was to his side, and started to pull it down. Suddenly, greenish light from the aurora sky began to cascade on us, drowning the soft light beam falling through the wall opening. I looked up in a jiffy and saw the small portion of that attic roof opening while Joe pulled that rope. For a moment, I felt that I was in a completely different world because what I could see above was truly unbelievable!

Twinkling stars were spread all over the sky and greenish aurora light made its way down to us through the leaves and branches of that tree. Under that glittering green aurora light, there appeared numerous bird nests all over those branches. With that breathtaking spectacle above, I kept gazing upward in astonishment with hands over my cheek.

'Welcome to the bird world,' said Joe with a gentle voice.

I said nothing. I was awestruck.

Seeing those many nests atop raised a curiosity in me. So, I stood up from the bed carefully, without bumping my head onto those branches above. Slowly, Joe also got up from that bed.

Now we both were on our feet, standing upon the bed, and surrounded by the branches with birds' nests all over. I was amazed at seeing the bird kingdom around me.

'Wow. What a place! This is so.....' Joe interrupted me from speaking further, shutting my mouth with his hand, as my loud voice made the birds chirrup in panic.

'Ssh.... Speak quietly.' Joe whispered with his hand over my lips.

He kept staring into my eyes with his hand over my lips. Under the glow of greenish aurora sky, Joe's face seemed sensual. His hand gently moved towards my left cheek from lips. Caressing my cheek, Joe slowly came close and kissed my lips. His kiss didn't arouse me, maybe because of the irritation during menstruation. He stripped my top while kissing. I felt thrilled at being semi-nude in front of Joe in the midst of such beauty with birds all around.

But immediately, a few bothering thoughts struck my mind. . . 'Does he want to have sex now? Oh no, how can I contribute in the time of this freaking menstruation?'. . . Because of these thoughts, my thrilling experience sank at once.

Joe's looks fixated on my cleavage with great passion. His lips reached there and ran all around my bra. Unhooking the bra, Joe kissed my nipples. He slowly moved downward and tried to pull my pant. Immediately, I shoved him back. Joe was baffled with my act.

'No Joe, not now.' I said in a low pitch tone, while pulling the bra back to my breasts.

'Why!' Joe whispered in the same baffle.

'I'm in period. Please I can't,' I said uneasily and sat down on the bed.

After some silence, Joe settled beside me and offered the unwrapped top. I took my top from him and wore it.

'I'm sorry... Our meet will happen only when you desire.' Joe said, suppressing disappointment.

I felt so thankful for his respectful behaviour and understanding nature.

'Thank you, Joe. Thank you for understanding.' I said.

Joe smiled.

His smile clearly lacked its usual honesty. I felt so bad for smashing Joe's desire and slammed the bloody nature for causing menstruation at this time.

Because of the precious moment that we missed, I craved it to happen on a special occasion that would remain an unforgettable memory in our lives. For this, I planned our copulation on my birthday night at Geiranger fjords which was 130 km away from Volda. I have a deep emotional connection with that place because I celebrated my birthday there every year with my family when we were united. So, I wished to celebrate my birthday with Joe in that beautiful place after many long years. As my birthday was just about to come in 9 days, I eagerly waited for the precious moment which was about to happen. I decided to keep my plan and even my birthday a secret from Joe to surprise him at once.

SOMETHING FISHY

Joe remained confined to the island and kept working on his childhood painting. But he felt that the emotion in his childhood face was not turning out as desired. Joe wanted to depict his joyful face from his childhood memory but could not.

I suggested that if we could go out and do painting sessions by observing the joyful faces of kids, that could make the painting work. But Joe did not show any interest to step out of the island.

As Joe was a renowned celebrity, I thought he was worried about showing himself in public.

I tried to convince Joe that nobody could recognize him in this altered look. So, we can make the painting outdoors without facing any trouble from the people.

But Joe was adamant and continued to paint in the island.

One day, inside Joe's painting studio, I discovered a sketch book containing numerous sets of eye sketches. Initially, I did not pay detailed attention to those eyes and kept flipping through the pages. But suddenly, I felt something common in all those sketches. There was a small mole beneath the corner of the left eyebrow in every sketch. This reminded me of my mole which I have at the same place beneath my left eyebrow. When I carefully read those eyes, I realized that all those sketches were depicting the joyful emotion in my eyes. I was stunned at finding those many sketches of my eyes. I was so curious to know the reason behind these sketches. So, I went to Joe with that book.

'I found this in the painting room. It contains many sketches of my eyes. Why did you draw them?' I asked, pointing to that sketch book.

'Cheerful emotions in your beautiful eyes could impel me to depict the true joy in the eyes of my childhood painting. This is the reason why I drew these.' Joe replied tentatively with his head down.

I then understood why he constantly kept looking into my eyes since our first meeting. He observed emotions in my eyes during those times and drew these sketches later in secrecy. But strangely, Joe never said about these sketches to me until I queried him. This clearly stated his inexpressive nature.

As days went by, alongside his inexpressive nature, I also noticed a strange mentality of Joe. He hadn't shown any interest in stepping out from the island and he was completely reluctant to meet new faces, even granny at home. This raised many doubts in me, suggesting that Joe was going through some significant issues.

'Why are you confined to the island? I can't understand why you are so reluctant to meet my people?' I questioned Joe, irked.

Joe went silent at my question.

Because of his silence, my frustration increased.

'Speak out... What's your problem in meeting my people?' I queried him in frustration.

'How can I...? Being a celebrity, it's not easy for me to come out and mingle with new people.' Joe replied in rage and walked away from me.

I could understand Joe's problem of being a public figure. But at the same time, I strongly suspected that there was something beyond this that Joe was not sharing. It didn't take a long time for this suspicion to come true. . .

DEVASTATION

One day... As Joe's old painting, which showed him playing music on piano, wore off its fragrance, Joe decided to refill it. Picking up 'Lily of the valley' flower's scent, Joe began spraying it on that painting. I felt curious about what made Joe use this scent in the painting? With this curiosity, I asked, 'Joe... What is the reason to choose this specific fragrance for this painting?'

'Lily of the valley flowers symbolize absolute purity. So to describe my pure love for music, I used the scent of this flower in this painting that shows me making music,' Joe said.

'Wow! That's really nice,' I admired.   I then questioned, 'Joe, why are you so desperate for the Diamond of Kinabalu orchid? Like the Lily of the valley flowers scent, do you want to use the Diamond of Kinabalu orchid's scent in any of your paintings?'

'Yes, my ongoing Childhood painting needs Diamond of Kinabalu orchid's fragrance,' replied Joe.

'Is it? What inspired you to choose that fragrance?'   I asked.

'Diamond of Kinabalu orchid's fragrance itself is an important element in my childhood incident because I sensed it all across the location while I was chasing butterflies. That lovely scent generated a pleasant mood in me. I want to define that pleasant mood of mine with those flowers' scent in the painting. I can also define the background location smell in the painting with this scent. That's why I am so desperate to get those flowers.'   Joe explained.

Upon hearing this, I understood Joe's need for this plant and why he was asking for it since our first meeting. As I came to know the importance of Diamond of Kinabalu orchid fragrance in Joe's ongoing painting, I intensified the search. I inquired about this rare plant in renowned botanical gardens and nurseries through emails and phone calls, but the authorities of those botanical gardens and nurseries confirmed that they did not have this plant. Aston tried to get it from the smugglers but failed. After these failed attempts, Joe sent Aston to Borneo 'Malaysia', native place for this flowering plant, to find it.

On the other hand, I decided to search for these flowers in local flower shops and nurseries. When I asked Joe to come along, he refused and insisted that I found them by myself. I rejected Joe's proposal and committed to find those flowers only with him. My intention was to make him step out of the island, so that we can have some good times outdoors. Because of my persistence Joe succumbed. So, he finally agreed to step out during the night.

I was more than happy to take Joe out. We had some good time by driving across the beautiful locations. I searched for those flowers in every flower shop that we had found on the way and also in the local nurseries, (Joe refused to step out and stayed within the car during these times). I didn't force Joe to get down because I understood his concern. Our search continued the following night. But I didn't manage to find those flowers.

Third night of our search was a special one, because my birthday was about to come in a few hours. After failing to find the plant, Joe decided to go to the island and I took the steering wheel. As per my plan, I drove towards Geiranger instead of going to the island.

'Hey... This is not the way to the island. Where are you going?' Joe questioned.

'We are going to Geiranger.' I replied.

'What...' Joe said in shock.

'Tomorrow is my birthday. I want to spend this precious occasion with you in Geiranger fjords.' I revealed my desire.

'No Cherry. I don't want to go there. Drive back to the island.' Joe said in vex.

'Shut up and stay quiet.' I countered.

'Cherry... Stop the car... Stop the car...' Joe shouted in anger.

'Joe please... I am doing so much for you, right. Can't you fulfill this small wish of mine?' I asked emotionally in a tender tone, holding his hand.

My emotional appeal made Joe silent. Although he was reluctant to go there, he did not oppose me anymore. I felt happy for Joe for not going against my wish and took him to that place.

After reaching Geiranger by 11:15 in the night, I kept driving the car in search of the right place for our stay. Far away from the Geiranger village, in the remoteness of the fjords, I found some vacant places at the shore of the water body. Convinced that this will be the perfect place to spend the special night, I stopped the car at the shore. Getting down from the car, I walked to its boot and started unloading the camp tent, frying pan, cooking ingredients, sliced pieces of salmon and other packed stuff from it.

'What the hell! When did you load all these into my car?' Joe asked, baffled at seeing the stuff.

'I gave the car key to your security officer at the coast building and asked him to load these.'

'Oh, so you pre planned this.' Joe said, irritated.

'Come on Joe.... I planned this to surprise you. Let us celebrate my birthday together.'

'You are truly insane,' said Joe in annoyance.

I put the tent and lit up a campfire in front of it using some dry sticks and wooden logs. Then I started preparing seared salmon with lemon butter and cream sauce for dinner on that fire. During this time, Joe remained inside the camp tent by puffing cigar nervously.

'Joe, come out and help me in preparing dinner,' I asked.

Puffing the cigar, Joe stayed silent inside that tent by looking at me angrily.

'Ok. I'm sorry to plan this without telling you. Please show some smile on your face.' I begged in a pleading tone.

But there was no smile on his face except nervousness and anger. Understanding Joe's moodiness, I continued to cook by myself.

After 30 minutes, I finished cooking. Inside the tent, we both started having that soft puffy salmon recipe along with a glass full of red wine. Meanwhile, my watch turned the date to 24 October and it was my birthday.

'Huhoooo.... I turned 28.' I said excitedly with a loud tone.

Joe didn't even wish me and continued to eat in a vexed manner.

'Joe, do you know something? I love this place so much. Long ago my family owned a small house in this village. We used to visit here every year on this day to celebrate my birthday. I had many memorable moments in this gorgeous place. But after my family split up, we sold off the house and I never came here thereafter. Now, I got an opportunity to spend some time with you here. Tell me, what shall we do after finishing dinner?' I asked Joe and waited for his reply in a wish to have sex.

'Let us go back to the island.' Joe replied against my wish.

'Oh, come on... It's my birthday. Do you want to constrain me behind the walls of the island on this special occasion?' I asked Joe with a bit of a disappointing tone.

Joe took a deep breath in vexation and continued to have dinner.

I saw a tiny piece of food stuck to his moustache. Looking at it, I kept my plate aside. I reached so close to Joe and removed that piece of food with my lips.

'Now I'm not in period. Nothing can stop us now.' I whispered with an impish smile and kissed Joe.

I completely pulled off his hoodie and found a tattoo of a bird with broken wings over his chest. I kissed his chest all over that tattoo. Joe didn't show any interest in proceeding further, maybe because he was angry at me for bringing him there against his wish.

But I didn't let down my momentum. I continued to kiss him all over and aroused him. Finally, Joe joined in. He shut the zipper of that tent. The burning fire outside that semi-transparent tent provided enough light to see each other. He then stripped off my clothes including my inner wear. I lied down in front of Joe in complete nudity. I felt truly excited. He pulled down his pants and I saw his bare body in underwear. Wow! His mesomorph body looked so eye-catching.

He lied on me and kissed my lips. For a while, we continued to smooch so deeply. His lips felt so warmth and his beard kept tickling me. He slowly came down to my neck and ran his tongue all over. I then felt his lips reaching further down to my breasts and my heartbeat increased rapidly. He kissed all over my breasts and damped my nipples with his saliva. I was no more in control and cuddled him in great pleasure. His play did not stop there, he went further down and kissed my privates. Feeling that heavenly pleasure, my eyes went shut automatically and I moaned by grabbing his hair firmly between my legs. 'Oh.... Please, keep on doing this,' I silently said within me while submerging in that lovely pleasure. He did it for the following 2 minutes which made me so aroused. I reached a point where I could not even breathe because of the fire Joe aroused in me. I craved for our intercourse to quench that burning fire.

When Joe was about to pull down his underwear to meet me, his wrist watch rang a beeping alert. . . This was the moment when the cruel time started its play. . .

With that alert, I observed a sudden mood swing in Joe. In a split second, his romantic mood turned barbaric. Immediately Joe pulled up his clothes and started to suspect everything around in an utmost panic state.

'Cherry.... let us go from here. There is someone around us. They can reach here anytime. I can't take any chances when you are with me,' said Joe in a terrified state and started pulling me out of that tent.

I couldn't understand what the hell was going on with Joe. As I was completely nude by then, I only managed to pull up my pantie and bra in that absolutely chaotic situation.

Meanwhile, Joe's watch rang the same alert again. Listening to this, his panic multiplied even higher and he put all his strength in pulling me towards the car, completely ignoring that I was semi-nude. There was no time for me to think why Joe was suddenly behaving like this!

I was completely horrified by his behaviour. As Joe started pulling me towards the car with great force, I kept resisting him. But he was not in a controllable state anymore.

Unable to find any other way to control him, I slapped Joe as hard as I could. With this slap, Joe left my hand and suddenly turned silent. In this silence, his watch kept on to sound the alert. Joe looked all around and ran towards the car. Getting in, he fled away leaving me back in a semi-nude state, breaking my heart and desire into pieces on the special moment of my birthday.

What happened to Joe suddenly??? Why did he behave like that??? What made him so frightened??? There were only questions, but no answers. I did not even imagine that my suspicion that something was wrong with Joe would come true in such a terrible way. I was completely shattered after what he had done.

Pulling my clothes up in tears, I left for home by borrowing a taxi. Oh no, what I had planned, but what happened eventually! Why time played this horrible game with me! I was utterly furious with myself for loving Joe and decided to stay away from him.

JOE:

REMORSE

Around 36 thousand feet high, up in the vast skies, above the borders of Norway and Sweden, my mind, full of Cherry's thoughts, travelled much quicker than my private jet to reach her and to clean up its clanger. It had been nearly a month since Cherry had left me, and I can't take it anymore. Thousands of miles away from my homeland, in a densely populated city like Agra, I needed to find a way. A way that can make me reach Cherry. A way that can fill a hope in her to trust me.

Agra.... This Indian city was described as a city of love by historians. How strange was my situation! In the city of love, I need to fight for my love. In the city of love, I have to find a way to reach my love. Along with the legendary love stories of Agra, will my love story also remain a heartbreak? No, I should not let it happen. With this determination, I landed in Agra.

In this city, we hired a guest house which belongs to a Delhi based businessman who was closely associated with my father. Media broke the news that I had come to Agra. With this news, Cherry might have understood why I was here, and we got an email from her. . . The email mentioned, 'Though you reached Agra, you can never reach me. It's all over, and there is nothing between us now. I can never forgive you. I don't even want to see your face again. Don't waste your time trying to reach me'. . . Seeing this email, my heart sank in grief. My eyes couldn't control the tears. Well, it is not easy for Cherry to forgive me because of the unforgivable sin I committed.

But I didn't lose hope. We started our search. Aston inquired for Cherry at the botanical labs, marble stores as Cherry's father is a marble merchant, and even tried to trace her by lobbying with the immigration authorities but failed. We sent her many emails but didn't get any reply.

We spent the whole week trying to locate her but couldn't. I was completely agonized. But my determination did not let me give up. I decided to proceed further until I reached Cherry. So, I said to Aston, 'No matter how many times we fail, no matter how many hurdles come, we should reach Cherry. Let's intensify the search'.

Aston turned frustrated by listening to this. 'Hell… Cherry is avoiding us. Why can't you still understand this? She has no intention to meet you and that's why she didn't even reply to our emails. We can search for a missing person, but how can we search a person who is avoiding us?' Aston ranted at me.

These words from Aston made me understand Cherry's enraged stance towards me. "Augh… how can I reach Cherry? Even if I reach her, will she forgive me? To clear out Cherry's rage on me, what should I do?" I kept contemplating. Then, my mind suggested that winning her heart will be the only way to reach Cherry instead of searching for her. But how can I do that??? After thinking for a while, I found my change could be the only possible way to win her heart. For this, if I do something that Cherry never thought that I could do, she might be able to believe my change. So, I decided to take a bold step in my life….

I walked into Aston's room and asked him to turn on the live stream on his mobile. Aston was shocked at listening to this. He perplexedly turned on the live stream in his mobile and gave it to me.

Constraining all the fears within me, I looked at the camera and said, 'Cherry, you never hated me even when I caused all sorts of troubles to you. I still strongly feel that your rage and disgust was only against my disabilities and fears, but not over me. I will kill all my fears and stand tall in front of you as you desired. For this, I am doing a concert the upcoming Sunday night, by the name of 'WINNING YOUR SHATTERED HEART'. You yearned for me to step out from the island in the past. Now, I'm stepping into the light, I'm coming in front of you with the concert. I hope this change in me will patch up your shattered heart'.

Announcement of my concert sparked a great curiosity in the media and public. Even my father who was always time constrained due to business deals, decided to attend my concert by keeping all his commitments aside.

Concert day.... Determined to prove my change and knowing that Cherry will never forgive me if I fail the event, I got on stage with all my fears still intact. Concert began with 'A date with you' which was one of my previously composed songs. While performing the song, my mind let me down in every possible way. I couldn't battle against my worst fears, I utterly surrendered to them. My voice started to crumble. My body shivered violently followed by heavy sweating and nausea. I felt my head spinning. In this dizziness, I collapsed onto my knees. Suddenly, my vision blurred and experienced a warped image of the horde in front. Unable to sustain this terrifying moment, I puked on the stage.... Immediately, security rushed to the stage and escorted me off stage.

An hour after the failed concert....

While resting on my bed, weakened, my mind ran through my agonizing past which pushed me into these devastating fears. . . . As I was born in UK'S richest family, world had thought that I was the lucky one. This was true to some extent. But, aside from being rich, there was another nasty side in my life that this world had never seen. World did not know how my love for music and dad's greed of moneymaking made me a guinea pig. Nobody ever thought that I was battling against myself for my own freedom. Nobody ever thought that I was a victim of my own glory. Everyone thought that my life has all the glitz and glamor. But, alongside this glitz and glamor, my past was also accompanied with unendurable torment. . . .

HIDDEN PAGES OF MY PAST

CHILDHOOD - (ACHIEVEMENTS)

The only thing that this world knew about my personal life was my background. As everyone knows, I am the only child of a mighty corporate tycoon 'Mr. Jeffery Bell (Jeff)'. Legendary musician and corporate bigwig 'Mr. William Bell' is my grandfather. Apart from this information, the rest of every aspect in my life was a closed book.

Before exploring the hidden pages of my life, one should know what made me so special.... Every person's talent has its roots from his predecessors. My story was not a different one either. Art and music were in my blood, thanks to my mom and grandpa.

In the early years of my life, I grew up watching my mother, who was an artist. She had done her master's in fine arts from University of Oxford and dedicated her life to finding new modes in art.

Simultaneously, I also spent a huge amount of time alongside my grandfather who was a renowned musician, songwriter and singer in his mid 30's. But later, he gave up his passion to take up the family business due to the sudden death of his father. 35 years later, handing over the business to my dad and aunt, he spent a good amount of time composing music.

This environment at home made me follow my predecessors' footsteps. From age 5, I started to paint scenes and compose music at the luxury of my imperial estate. I constantly kept enhancing my painting and music skills with the help of my mom and grandpa.

My mother's style of painting was to use naturally made colours instead of fumed paints. In her intent, those naturally made colours were not only environmentally friendly, but also easy to work with. She took it a step forward and used perfumes in those colours to give a pleasant smell to her painting.

I adopted her style of painting by using those naturally made aromatic colours. But my distinguished little brain never stopped there. One day, mom was busy painting a portrait using natural colours blended with rose perfume. While inhaling that pleasant rose fragrance, my brain came up with an idea. . . 'Instead of using this fragrance in painting for no obvious reason, how would it be if I make that smell an important aspect in painting? So if I paint a rose flower using this fragrance, the painted rose smells like a real flower. Thus my painting can express the fragrance of a rose'. . .

With this idea, I immediately took some colours from mom's palette and rushed to my room. Sitting down, I started painting the rose flower.

Once completed, I reached back to mom. She was busy painting. Curiously, I patted her on the back. She stopped painting and turned at me.

'Hey Joe, what's that in your hand? Is that a new painting?'

'Yes mom. I painted a rose.' I said and showed it to her excitedly.

'Mmm! This looks great. Nice painting honey. You have done a good job,' mom said this by caressing my cheek.

Mom's compliment gave me great pleasure.

'Mom, once smell the painting,' I said and waited curiously for her response.

'Hmm, anything special?' asked mom.

'Yeah...' I nodded excitedly.

Mom sniffed the painting. At first, I did not observe any reaction in her face. I thought that she didn't catch my intention behind the painting. But a second later, mom's face showed surprise, sensing something different. Then, she sniffed the painting again. Immediately, her face was lit up with amazement.

'Oh my goodness...! This was emitting the fragrance of a rose flower. Did you paint this purposefully?' Mom asked with the same amazement.

Mom's recognition for my achievement and astonishment in her face brought instant happiness in me.

'Yes mom....' I replied blissfully, looking into her astounded face.

Mom knelt at me with a proud smile. 'I didn't get this idea in all these years. Honey, you are a genius,' Mom said this with a hug and kissed me.

This hearty reception and praise from mom made me so happy.

As time passed, with the help of my mother, I developed this new idea as my signature style by inducing smell to match, create, enhance or depict the mood in my paintings.

I didn't stop there either. I intended to bring my beloved music and painting together. I tried to blend them. Depending on the scene and mood in my immature paintings, I used to compose music with the help of my grandpa. With all these, my painting expressed smell, music and sounds evoking the mood in it.

I also made a few tunes exclusively without blending them with paintings. When I was 6, my mom introduced me to books. Reading stories, poems and fantasy from those books made me visualize and develop many new thoughts. I used to express those thoughts through my paintings and music. My days went smoothly back then.

Because of my talent in music, I stood as the centre of attraction at every singing program in my school events. At the time when everyone at school and in the mansion wondered at my talent in music at such a young age, dad started to see me in a totally different way....

Dad put my talent in front of the world by promoting me through his music company. I felt so grateful to dad for recognizing my love towards music and encouraging me on such a large scale. Because of dad's influence and having own music company, my entry to the music world became easy.

Just within days after my entry to the music world, summer break began. With no school, I wholly concentrated on music and started to attend studios for singing in albums.

Alongside singing, I also composed two albums with the backing from my grandpa.

Along with album recordings, I also started doing concerts. My tunes used to bring out all of London's music fans to fill up the concert halls. My unique style which I kept following in paintings was applied at my concerts as well. Auditoriums were filled with a particular fragrance to match the mood of my tune.

If the tune was pacy, fragrances of peppermint, orange scent, rosemary were used to elevate the energizing mood in spectators.

If it was a melodious tune, fragrances like vanilla, lavender, jasmine, champak flower scent and some specially made aromas were used to create a pleasant and relaxing mood.

My performances mesmerized spectators and my concerts became great success. My unique technique of elevating mood through aromas stood as a secret aspect in my concert triumphs.

My successful journey took a step ahead when dad's company sponsored a deal by collaborating me with Ryan, a renowned musician cum singer, for my upcoming albums. We both made three albums together that became enormous successes.

People started to talk more about my tone's domination in those albums while almost completely ignoring Ryan's tone and composition. I reached a level where Ryan's composition could not sustain without me. Even other music companies which were collaborating with Ryan, came to me by either cancelling those contracts or by asking me to collaborate with him. I agreed to those companies' proposals with the intent to spend more time in music. My time with music felt more enjoyable than my success.

CHILDHOOD - (SUFFOCATION)

After summer vacation, I went back to school. When I was walking through a corridor to reach my classroom, I noticed all the faces of my school mates were staring at me. Suddenly, they sprinted towards me and surrounded me in huge numbers. Some of them looked at me with great excitement and started to praise. I did not understand what was going on and was absolutely terrified by then. Meanwhile, Miss Lisa, my favourite teacher, separated them. She then escorted me towards my classroom. Reaching the class, I took my place.

'Edward, everyone was talking about your music. Truly, you are a wonder kid. I'm proud to be your teacher. Can I have your autograph?' Miss Lisa asked me to sign a book.

Her face and voice clearly expressed wonder at me while asking for my autograph. This perplexed me. I wondered why my beloved teacher suddenly behaving like this!

If a teacher asks her student to do something, how could he not do that? Feeling awkward in that perplexed state, I wrote my name on that book. . . That was my first autograph when I was just 6 years old. . .

After her exit, all other teachers came to my class at once and appreciated me for my achievements in music.

By seeing those teachers in such large numbers around me, I was utterly scared. All their compliments felt too heavy. All their astounded looks upon me seemed wild rather than appreciative. I felt so difficult to deal with my teachers. Unable to react in that awkward and scary situation, I held my fright within me and sat calmly by looking at them nervously.

It was my classmates turn after the teachers. My fellow mates with whom I spent all my school time previously, now suddenly started to treat me like a superhero. This sudden change of behaviour in them baffled me.

No class took place that day. In fact, I became the main topic to everyone in my class on that day. Because of this overwhelming reception, for the first time, school felt like a burden to me.

After finishing school, thinking about the abrupt change that happened to my people in the class, I stepped out of the school building. There I saw a group of my schoolmates waiting outside of the school's compound fence for their parents. Along with them, there were few parents who came to pick their kids. Upon seeing me, people in that group started murmuring at each other with great excitement in their faces. Some of them stared intensely at me with surprised faces and remaining gestured 'Hi.....' at me with great enthusiasm. I knew few people in that group, as they were my friends and their parents. I interacted with them many times in the past. But I never saw this kind of excitement upon seeing me.

All the mess that I had been going on since morning had felt so strange and burdensome to me. My little brain did not understand why everyone was behaving that way? It felt like an enigma. I couldn't know why people suddenly started to treat me so specially!!!

Because of their pointed looks towards me, I felt so timid. I stood at the front porch of the school building and never tried to step forward in fear of those people.

I looked all over that group for my mom who was supposed to pick me up. But she was nowhere to be seen. Waiting for her, I remained at the same place with my head down. Meanwhile, those outside people and other schoolmates gathered around me in large numbers, showing their excitement. Seeing them, I was absolutely petrified and didn't understand what to do! Like Miss Lisa did in the morning, no one came to separate them. It was a moment of terror and helplessness.

When I was in this utterly frightened state, mom reached me. All the fear and discomfort that gathered in me since morning suddenly dissipated upon seeing my mother. Immediately, I burst out in tears and hugged her. Mom knelt at me and wiped my tears by consoling me. Because of the people around me, she must have realized why I was in tears. Mom held me in her arms and carried towards the car by shoving the people to a side. Hiding my face behind her shoulder, I tightly closed my eyes. I did not even dare to open my eyes to see what was going on around with the people. That day was a terrible one at school.

Same like in school, I noticed a drastic change in people's behaviour whenever I was out to have some jolly time. Like others, there was no scope for me to eat ice cream in the streets, go shopping, or to enjoy in the playgrounds. Because, each time people irritated me by gathering around with wild excitement. Their adulation used to make me so fearful. That was the time when my little brain started to understand what stardom was and how heavy it will be to carry.

Apart from my gifted artistry and fame, I was just like any other kid who wanted to have a merry time with fellow mates, play silly games in the open fields, build sand castles, chase squirrels and cause every other mischief. But these desires were taken away from me so quickly....

Difficulties of fame continued at school with my own friends. In the past, I was one among others in my class. But now, I became the only one among others. I was not just another kid but a celebrity who shared the class with other six-year-olds. My friends treated me like a demigod, rather than their fellow friend. Because of this, I could not tolerate them and detached from them. I showed no interest in mingling with them again because of their overwhelming behaviour. My solitude felt very pleasant when compared to the encircling of my friends.

While fellow mates of mine were playing outside, I constrained myself to the walls of my classroom. From my empty classroom, I watched in solitude as they enjoyed themselves. My heart craved so much to be a part of those laughs and happiness but could not. I knew what would happen once I stepped there. I will become the centre of attraction to them and their congregation around me could only cause great tribulation rather than joy.

While my social life was going through these difficulties, my success showed me absolute horror....

Dad's music company sponsored my collaborating concert with Ryan. This was the biggest event to be held in London in recent times. Dad's intent was to promote me much further through this concert. Twickenham stadium was to host this great event. And I had to sing my previously made songs on stage along with Ryan.

Concert day

As the songs were a bit pacy, I chose rosemary fragrance to raise the energizing mood in the crowd. While aroma diffusers (which were fitted around the stadium) emitted the fragrance of rosemary all over, I occupied the stage along with Ryan and the orchestra. There were approximately a hundred thousand people in front of us, which made me anxious. Gathering all my courage, I started to perform nervously alongside Ryan.

As the concert went on, the crowds went crazy, cheering me on. Those cheers dissipated my anxiety and boosted me up. This sparked a spirit of enthusiasm in me and I continued to sing with utmost grace....

Once the concert ended, the entire Twickenham stadium echoed with the loud praises of '....Edward Bell..... Edward Bell...... Edward Bell....'

Listening to the praises, applause and roars from the horde, my heart filled with delight. It brought an instant smile on my lips. Big screen in that stadium displayed my smiling face in full glory. . . 'That was the last time I smiled heartily. I have never had a smile on my face again'. . .

After receiving all the praises and applause from the horde, I went to rest in my private dressing room. In the solitude of that room, I sat on the couch and closed my eyes. My mind felt the calmness of that room, as there were no roars of crowd.

A minute later, I heard the door opening. I opened my eyes and saw Ryan entering my room. He shut the room's door and locked its bolt. His body language seemed somewhat shady. Upon seeing him, I stood from the couch and smiled in greeting. But he did not smile back. Slowly striding towards me, he reached me and knelt in front of me. Expression in his face felt strange. I did not understand whether that expression was anger or poise!

'Edward Bell.... Edward bell.... My ears still ring with this praise from the crowd,' Ryan with the same strange expression, said in a low pitch tone while patting my cheek.

His pat on my cheek felt harsh, and not appreciative. Ryan got up and turned away from me. I thought he was going from my room. But suddenly, he turned at me and banged me to the floor. I was absolutely terrified by his awful act. In a moment of dread and pain, I started to sob.

'Shut your mouth, you bloody little bastard.' Ryan ranted and blocked my mouth with his hanky.

I kept on wailing. But no sound came out from my gagged mouth. He then picked me up from the floor with force and tied my hands back with his belt. Grabbing my throat, Ryan banged my head against the table.

'How I used to be but how you changed my life in just three months. You took away all my contracts. You ruined my popularity. If I leave you like this, you will leave me to sell cakes and drinks in front of your concert halls.' Ryan said in fury by clenching his teeth.

He turned me around and made me lay flat on my stomach on that table. Applying all his strength, he squeezed my head towards the table. Feeling that pain, I wailed in agony. Using all my force, I tried to free myself but couldn't.

'I will not make you forget this throughout your life. You must suffer every minute by thinking about this. You deserve this for what you did to me,' Ryan said in a rage and pulled off my pants.

He then removed his pants. What he did to me then was unexplainable..... My little brain did not even understand what he was doing to me??? That pain felt like hell, and I kept screaming hard and hard and hard. But those screams didn't come out from my sealed mouth. He kept trashing my head to the table along with his terrorizing act. I could not breathe, and my head felt spinning because of thumping. Then, suddenly the back door of the room opened, and mom entered in. Upon seeing Ryan's brutal act on me, mom screamed in shock. With her presence, Ryan left me and pulled up his pants in panic. Following mom's scream, three private security officers reached the room. Seeing them, Ryan tried to flee away. But he was caught by those security officers. . . With this heinous act from Ryan, I thought for the first time that success had earned me nothing but pain and trouble. . .

I was utterly horrified and fazed by that incident. The terror Ryan left in my life was immeasurable. I even feared seeing people. Everyone around seemed like Ryan to my eyes in a devilish form. This fright did not let me step out of my room. In every dream at night, I recalled that nightmare. I completely succumbed to that excruciating trauma and could not get out of it....

Mom was heartbroken with my situation and feared the worst. She left the paint brush and devoted all her time to me. Her twenty four by seven presence and care reduced my panic. Whether it was day or night, I was too scared to be away from mom. Her presence and care felt less alone and much secure. Because of her love, I didn't drift into greater depths of distress...

Seeing me in anguish, mom assigned a counselling therapist at home itself. Alongside those counselling therapies, mom tried to improve my devastated mood by narrating many inspirational stories, encouraging me to listen to pleasant music, playing indoor games, and making me spend some time in painting. These efforts from mom kept me calm and deviated my mind from dreadful thoughts of Ryan...

On the other hand, counselling therapies filled a little courage to cope with this problem.

World did not know about the abuse I faced. Keeping in mind the family's honour, it was kept as a top secret. Because of this, there was no legal action against Ryan and he continued with his music.

On the other hand, my agonizing situation kept me away from the world and music.

Media started to question, 'Why was I being reclusive? And what's the reason to take a break from music?'

Then, dad's music company released a statement that I was facing some minor health issues and will be back soon.

Few days later, Ryan died in a car mishap. Everyone thought it was an accident. But mom strongly believed it was not just any accident! It was a pre-planned murder commissioned by dad! When mom raised this doubt, dad contradicted with her.

Was it an accident or murder??? No one knew the actual truth, except dad. But dad never opened his mouth about this matter again. Hence Ryan's death remained a big mystery.

7 weeks later....

Because of the support from mom and counselling therapies, I was feeling better and patched up.

But unlike mom, dad never cared about my condition and was busy with his business empire. He spent most of his time administering his companies, rather than staying with me during this turbulent time. Because of this stance from dad, I was stuck in a perplexed state, thinking what was wrong with him?

One night, a question arose in me just before sleep, 'Why was dad not beside me? Was his business more important to him than me?' While I was pondering about this, dad visited me after calling it a day at work. His arrival was going to answer my question. But that answer was totally different from what I initially thought about him....

'Hey honey, It's exciting news. I brought a new sponsorship deal for you.' Dad, who sat next to me on the bed, said this by ruffling my hair.

As soon as I heard these words from dad, I could not understand how to react! It was a moment of exhilaration along with fear in me. I felt happy to resume my music soon. At the same time, I also feared what atrocities will success bring once I restart music?

While I was stuck in this state, mom who was beside me, took dad out of the room in rage and shut the door.

'This is ridiculous. How can you do this Jeff? Can't you see Joe's condition? Enough.... please stop it here. Joe will not continue music anymore.' Mom's irate voice reached my ear from the other side of the room.

'What? Joe is not like any other kid Elin. Can't you recognize his talent? Moreover, he was making millions for the company, how can I leave him.' Dad countered.

'How can you talk like this...? He's our child. Will you trade his happiness to increase your wealth? I cannot let it happen Jeff. I will not allow him to continue music.'

'Do you fear that incident? Ok, I can assure that no one can create any further problems to Joe,' said dad.

'It is not only about someone who could create problems. It's also about Joe's stardom. He was unable to bear that burden in this age. I can clearly understand that, but why can't you...?' Mom's tone raised in frustration.

'Do you think fame is a burden? You know how many people were craving for such fame? Once come out and see how fondly everyone was talking about our child,' Dad's angry tone hit back at mom.

'But what did it bring Joe? What did it bring us, except seeing him in this miserable condition,' said mom in agony.

'It brought him status. It brought me money. Your bourgeois mentality cannot understand the importance of fame and status... Listen Elin, as soon as Joe recovers, he has to continue music at any cost, even if he doesn't like it. No one can stop Joe from doing music, and it's better for you to not interfere in this matter.' Dad outrageously warned mom.

I then understood what I meant to my dad. Till then, I thought dad was supporting me because he was proud of my music. But that's when I realized that he was intent on increasing his wealth in every possible way and put me in the market as an aspect of moneymaking. It was clear for me that business was much more significant for him than me.

As dad said, mom could be from a middle class family. However, she was rich in heart and so she understood my odds. But dad's ever-growing wealth suggested the poor mentality of doing business on his own son.

Within 3 weeks, dad set everything to restart my music. But mom tried to put brakes on dad's efforts by motivating me otherwise.

'Continuing music will bring nothing but more trouble to you, Joe. It could only ruin your life further. Please concentrate on your personal life and studies first. Have a happy life like other kids. This is so important for you now. You can resume music once grown up.' Mom said with concern.

'There is nothing more important than music for me, mom. I cannot live without it. You are there to take care of my troubles. So why should I worry until you are with me,' I replied to mom.

Mom went silent. Maybe, my words made see my love for music and my trust on her to take care of my worries.

Though I understood dad was greedy on making money over me, I didn't care and resumed music, because I was so fascinated to spend time in it. The only worry for me was mom. I thought that she will resist this move. But thankfully, she didn't.

When I stepped back into the world, people and paparazzi kept gathering around me wherever I was, whether it was in front of recording studios or elsewhere. By seeing them around, mental scars created by Ryan kept showing their effects on me. My fear and rage weren't constrained only to Ryan. It also spread to this nasty world while encountering people's craziness for me. Everyone around me seemed so wicked, same as Ryan, while they were falling over themselves for my autographs and photographs. This freaking behaviour of people used to generate great unease and anxiety in me. All their pointed looks felt as ferocious as Ryan's looks at the time of abuse. I did not see any difference between people and Ryan. If Ryan abused me sexually, people's adulation and madness kept abusing me mentally. This psychological abuse from people felt more agonizing than Ryan's sexual abuse. Because it kept following me everywhere, it constantly intruded my privacy and freedom. Because of these experiences, I became fearful of people. I could not do anything other than hate people for causing this torture to me.

I could not come to terms with these difficulties in my life and nothing seemed to change in my school. All my fellow mates continued to treat me the same. They had already forgotten that I was a fellow classmate. Here I belong to everyone, except myself. I was absolutely devastated and kept myself away from them like I did in the past. But they didn't leave me alone and kept invading my privacy incessantly. . . 'I don't need hero-worship from you people.... Please leave me alone,' I struck back at my friends. . . But no one cared about my feelings. I totally forgot the word called freedom in my school life and every passing day caused unbearable burden. Because of this hero-worship, I was utterly outraged with my fellow mates and couldn't control my emotions. So, I kept getting into fights. This gave me a bad boy image at school, and teachers kept complaining about my rude behaviour. These constant struggles filled hatred and fear in me towards school. Therefore, I refused to attend school.

Mom put me in another school. But the same difficulties persisted there as well. What I understood was that problems would not resolve by changing schools. Whatever school it would be, my stardom would follow me wherever people are. So I quit school. Mom became utterly furious with my move. She forced me to quit music, but not school. I felt my life without music was nothing. Time with music felt so compelling and time without it was a hassle. So I brushed aside mom's demand and continued music.

While I was going through these difficulties with people, dad's company sponsored another concert of mine....

When I got on to the stage at the time of this concert, my fear of people started to show its cruelty on me because of the massive hordes in front of me. The entire horde started roaring and cheering me as I settled on stage. Unlike previously, their roars and cheers felt extremely horrifying rather than uplifting. The whole scene sent a shiver down my spine. I felt stomach popping out of my mouth. My sight was completely filled with that massive horde and every person in that horde seemed like a demon. Their gaze seemed so devilish and their horrendous screams raised my fear to zenith. That terrifying experience blurred my vision and my head started spinning. Suddenly, I felt I was losing my balance and those demons seemed rushing towards me at once. By experiencing this dreadful visual, I ran off stage, yelling with fear.

I sprinted into my dressing room and sat down at the corner in a terrorized state. Everything around seemed spinning and the boos of the masses kept ringing in my ears from outside that room. Unable to tolerate that spinning sensation and boos, I closed my eyes and ears tightly in fright.

A while later, I felt someone's hands touching my shoulders. Sensing that touch, I let my hands down from my ears and opened my eyes. As soon as I opened my eyes, I saw a blurry image of dad.

'What happened Joe...!' Along with the boos from outside, I heard dad saying this.

I couldn't respond to dad in that frightened state.

Slowly dad's hand moved from my shoulder to cheek. 'Hey honey... look... look here... can you hear me?' said dad, patting my cheek.

This touch over my cheek felt the same as Ryan's touch at the time of abuse. Suddenly, my mind suggested something bad was going to happen again. Seclusion from that room and ambience just like in the past had strengthened this apprehension. At this moment, dad's face seemed more threatening than ever before. Upon seeing dad's face, the fear running within me had erupted out in the form of a loud scream. My breath got stuck in terror. I felt I was losing consciousness and my eyes were closed. Within a second, my body hit the floor and the crowd's horrendous noises from outside went mute....

When I regained consciousness, I was moved to home and the concert got cancelled. I feared to be with dad, because the feeling that he was going to do something bad to me still didn't leave my mind. This fear of dad had gone with the passing time. But fear of people didn't leave me....

After that awful experience, I refused to do any other concert. This fear of people kept growing with every passing day. And to avoid them, I started to attend studios only during late nights for my recordings and shoots. Silence and peace of nights, less number of technicians around, absence of fans and paparazzi in front of studios made me to concentrate on music without any unnecessary worries.

Except for attending studios, I showed no interest in stepping out of the mansion. My solitude at the mansion felt so heavenly that I did not see myself being with people. Gradually, solitude became a major part of my life and all my previous struggles with people made me disown society. This hatred of people made its way to canvas in the form of paintings. I kept my painting skill so confidential from the world because I didn't want to get fame in painting like in music.

As days went by, I completely banished society and all social activities like outings and school from my life....

CHILDHOOD - (MOM'S COMFORT)

Over the time, mom saw how much I enjoyed music and allowed me to continue with my passion. She tried to set the things right in my life rather than to keep me away from music....

Mom understood that I was reluctant to attend school in fear of people and came up with an alternative. She assigned a set of teachers to teach me all the necessary curriculum at home without the crowded environment of school.

Mom didn't stop there. She kept pushing me to find my vanished freedom and move out from closed doors. Firstly, mom took me to an amusement park. But I couldn't pluck up the courage to step out of the car in fear of people around. Next day, early in the morning, mom took me to the beautiful landscapes outside of London. Far away from people, in those secluded landscapes, I experienced the beauty of nature during dawn after a long time. Nature's sounds such as whispering wind, floating water, birds chirping, and the sound of moving grass felt so relaxing in the calmness of those beautiful surroundings. It sounded like nature was expressing itself in the form of this music. The distress accumulated in the layers of my heart, eased a bit while listening to this pleasant music. 'Wow.... is there any music as alluring as this? Surely not.' I felt while listening to that peaceful music from nature.

Putting down the soft top of the car and enjoying nature's music in those secluded landscapes, I steered the car by sitting in mom's laps. On that day, for the first time in my life, I observed different types of birds which were present all around. I don't know why? But I liked watching birds fly.

Slowly, with the passing days, birding became my hobby. I started to detect bird species simply by hearing their chirps, without even seeing them. Alongside birding, watching them flying in vast skies captivated my heart so deeply. Well, why not! Freedom and happiness were lacking in my bitter life it was natural that I was soothed a bit by watching them fly joyfully with freedom. 'Oh, when can I experience such joy and freedom in my life? When will my agonizing life give me such a chance???' My heart yearned while watching them flying.

Recognizing my keen interest towards birding, mom never missed taking me out in the mornings. Apart from birdwatching, I loved to drive the car. So, I continued to learn driving with mom's help.

Seeing my loneliness at home, mom gave me a puppy. But I showed no interest to be with it or play with it. Because that puppy seemed like a prisoner alongside me in my confinement.

Then, being aware of my love towards birds, mom gifted me a Blue Tit bird. That bird stayed with me for more than 3 weeks in its cage. But seeing that bird's captivity in that cage, I started feeling guilty. . . . 'My life was anyhow limited because of my stardom. But why should I confine this poor bird to a cage? Was this suggesting my envy towards this bird which could fly joyfully with freedom?' I questioned myself in guilt.

Being aware from my own experience how miserable it will be to ruin one's freedom and happiness, I did not wanted that bird to be in captivity anymore. So, I let the bird out from that cage. Seeing that bird flying out gave me so much more pleasure than seeing it beside me in a cage.

That evening a wonderful thing happened in my life. The bird I let free came back to me again. I don't know why. Maybe, she saw my loneliness from that cage! Maybe, she thought of being my companion in my solitude!

From that day, she became my dearest friend. I didn't keep her in any cage. Instead, I made a small wooden nest house for her. I even named her Bluety (due to its colour and beauty).

Every morning, Bluety used to go out. . . I felt Bluety's freedom as mine while seeing her fly out of my room. I felt Bluety's joy as mine while watching her flying happily in the skies. I simply felt like her because my distressing life didn't give me an opportunity to have my own freedom and joy. . . My room's window was always kept open for her arrival in the evenings. When she arrived, two of us use to spend some playful time together. Her 'Tee... Tee...' sounds and naughty actions caused me some pleasure, forgetting my worries.

With the passing days, I kept myself within my room with activities like practicing music, painting my feelings, reading books, writing poetry and playing with Bluety. When life was calming down after all of the turbulence, another wonderful thing happened to me....

Feeling that I was lacking a companion, mom assigned Aston Langer. He was the son of Justin Langer, who was a loyal PA to my dad. As Aston lost his mother at a very young age, and Justin Langer was always busy assisting my dad, Aston spent most of his time with me in the mansion. He accompanied me to my private class and to my recording studios as well.

Aston understood me quicker than any other kid our age. Unlike my friends at school, he didn't treat me as a special person. This attracted me towards him. With the passing time, he became everything to me. Aston was the only person after mom, to whom I could express all my personal feelings. I felt him like my brother from another mother. Seeing our bond, mom was so happy for us.

These moves from mom provided a bit of serenity in my distressed life. Because of her, I have Aston and Bluety in my life. I even have outings to watch birds flying. Moreover, how can I forget her succour during my turbulent times. Without mom, my life would have been nothing. I would have succumbed to that torment and could never have come out of it. I didn't understand how to thank her for all these. This gratitude towards mom made my relationship more affectionate towards her.

TWEEN - (STRANGULATION)

5 Years later

For many people, things may move so quickly in five years. But in my case, nothing seemed to have changed. In all these years, my life was just limited to studios, home and some outings with mom during mornings....

Although my personal life was not good all these years, I felt somewhat relieved from that agony because of music. I composed many albums during this time and most of them had great success. Successful outcome of these albums encouraged me to do something differently. Since I started music, I have worked on Jazz, Classical, Electronic, Soul and Pop. Now, I intended to try something new and wrote a slow pace song which depicted the divinity in being alone.

Song:

Where can you find yourself
Where can you be yourself
Where can you do everything you wished to do....
Only when your alone.

Your solitariness is your true consort
It been with you since you are in womb
It comes with you even to the eternal rest
Why to crave for bonds in the middle.
Forget the pain of not having anyone
And start flying in the amity of yourself.

Listen to the chirps of the birds
Listen to the sound of the breeze
And ignore the noise of the horde until you reach a distant paradise.
Where you can find yourself
Where you can be yourself
Where you can do everything you wished to do'

While thinking how freshly I can compose this song, spending some private time in nature during mornings and listening to nature's music ignited something new in my brain. . . 'As nature's sounds sounded like pleasant music to my ear, how would it be if I made music using those sounds?'. . . I felt that the nature's enticing sounds could describe one's peace of mind while being alone. I also believed that those sounds would help in creating a pleasant mood to this newly written song.

There were genres like New age music and Bio music, using nature's sounds since many decades. Whether it's New age music or Bio music, the main purpose for using nature's sounds was to create a relaxing mood for the listener. But instead of relaxation, I intended to use these sounds to reflect the album's protagonist's heavenly mood who lives alone in a beautiful vast nature far from the world.

Matching to the written song, I selected sounds like, chirping of different birds especially nightingale, canary and rose-breasted grosbeak, whispering wind and sound of moving grass. To create a celestial mood in the song, I used piano, violin, flute and fused them with soft electronic music, light music and nature's sounds. After composing music, I sang the song with a mellifluous voice without sudden loud chords. Once the song was combined with the composed music, as a final touch, I gave a slight echo to my tone to create a pleasant haunting experience.

Ultimately, the song sounded harmonious and sweetly haunting. Instruments, sounds and my tone in the song, represented the peacefulness of my solitude. I was so happy because the song was resembling my nature and state of mind.

Once the song was done, I felt vast isolated grassy uplands will be the perfect location to shoot the song for getting a solitary feeling in the visuals. Since the past 5 years, I have only visited the studio settings to picturize my albums in fear of people. Now, the content and brilliance of my newly composed song got me to think of going against my fears. But I was not in a situation to take an audacious step to go out for shooting the song.

While I was ambiguous about going out for shooting the song or to choose some alternative, my brain came up with an idea. . . 'Instead of choosing some other grassy uplands, how would it be if I shoot the song in my family's owned farms in the Southern Uplands of Scotland?'. . .

This idea seemed great. So, we reached there to shoot the song. Since the farm was ours, it provided me complete privacy from people without facing any hardships from them.

Away from people, maintaining the secrecy, our team started to shoot the song with me. I was the only character to appear in the album because the song defined the divine nature of solitude. According to the mood and slowness of the song, I designed the visuals at a slow pace. Once everything was done, the song seemed so different from the rest of my albums. I was so happy for such a fine exhibition of work.

The song was named 'Edward Bell's - Alone'. When this song hit the market, it created a new history with the sales of over 38 million copies just in a period of 2 weeks, listing top as a best seller in less time and one of the bestselling singles of all time. Many articles described the song as a trance. World started to praise my work as a masterpiece and gave me the title 'Little legend'. In no time, this specific style of New age music became a new phenomenon called 'Edwardzee'. Many contemporaries of mine started to follow this unique style.

As my popularity rose to apex, my personal life started to deteriorate even more. Because of fans' craziness and the following of paparazzi in the past, I made a habit of attending studios only at night to escape from them. But now, media entered this list to intrude my freedom even at nights....

During my first visit to the studio after the great success of my song, I saw media reporters encircling my car in front of the studio. Seeing them from such a close distance made my blood curdle. All their faces looked shady while staring towards my car. My workplace which I treated as a shrine, now seemed like hell with the presence of the reporters.

'Augh... did these fuckers decided to invade my privacy even in the nights???' Voice of my mind wailed in agony.

Anticipating some kind of mess from them, I was not brave enough to step out of the car and closed its window curtains. As I was scared to get down the car, Aston who was sitting beside me, called for help. Within a minute, security guards of that studio reached the car. In the presence of those security guards, my chauffeur opened the door. While I was getting down the car, reporters fell over me and started asking, 'Edward Edward Edward.... What is your feeling about the great success of your song? What is your word to the people for making your song such a big hit? And blah-blah-blah....'

Pushing the reporters aside, security guards safeguarded me towards the studio. But they kept asking questions and followed me like vultures to eat my flesh. Feeling terrified and disgusted, I ignored the reporters and entered the studio in the protection of those security guards.

While walking towards the recording room, on the wall of honour, I saw photographs of legendary musicians along with their signature on the label just beneath their photo frames. I had seen this honours wall many times when I was in this studio previously. But now, to my surprise, I discovered my photograph alongside those legends on the honours wall. But it didn't give me any contentment. Instead, the only thought that sparked in my mind was. . . 'Will the times be much worse than before due to this legendary status? Does the evil experience with the media outside indicate this?'. . .

With this apprehension running through my mind, my heart felt that the upcoming times could be much more miserable than the past days. 'Oh no, how strange is fate in my case!!! Everyone's life will disintegrate with their failures. But bizarrely, my life disintegrated because of my enormous success'.

When I was immersed in these gloomy thoughts, I saw the empty label beneath my photograph. In a dejected mood, I picked up a pen from my pocket. Instead of putting my signature, I drew a bird with broken wings on that label, 'Describing that my fame, which had amplified due to this legendary status, can smash my wings and make me unable to obtain any freedom and joy'.

After drawing, I walked into the recording room. But those disturbing thoughts about my future didn't give me any chance to involve myself in my work....

Next day... Fate had never shown mercy over me. This time it mangled me with an irreparable blow.

It was a weekend and it was a day off for me from recording. Typically at every weekend night, there will be some party in the mansion with dad's opulent guests and this weekend was no exception. Whenever there was a party, I would go to bed earlier than normal to keep myself away from the guests....

While I was in deep slumber, my ears sensed a huge thump sound from somewhere! Suddenly, I woke up to that heavy sound. The sound told me that something had happened that was not supposed to. I slowly got up from bed in a drowsy state and opened my room's door. As soon as I opened the door, I saw subordinates and guests running downstairs in a state of shock. Seeing this, I felt something went terribly wrong! Immediately, a worry kicked in me. Holding my nerve, I followed them downstairs. Reaching out of the mansion, I saw a bunch of guests and other mansion staff gathered around.

Atmosphere among them looked lament. Sensing this, my mind brewed up many bad thoughts. I gulped my throat in worry and walked towards those people. By shoving them aside, I made my way through them and reached forward. To my front, I saw the most dreadful and heart breaking visual of my life. Aside to the shattered whiskey glass and grieving dad, mom was lying motionless on the ground with blood all around. Her eyes were half open. Her face was bruised. Her arm was broken and completely turned over. Seeing mom in that condition, my heart crushed. It felt like a thousand typhoons striking the coast at once. Mom's blood slowly flowed towards me as a stream and touched my feet. I was absolutely horrified and moved my foot back. But the stream continued to flow towards me and touched my foot again. 'The blood which shared all the love and affection, couldn't leave me even at this time.'

'Jesus... How did this happen?' Subordinate behind me murmured with her fellow worker in a grief stricken tone.

'She accidentally fell down from the balcony while drunk.' That worker muttered to her.

Everyone around me looked shattered. Some of them were wailing. But, I didn't. I didn't because I was already numb by then. My brain had stuck with the distressing visual in front of me. I felt like time was frozen and the world stopped spinning.

With mom's demise, world around me was filled with emptiness. No one came close to filling this huge void. My solitude recalled mom with every ticking second. The fact that mom was no more had strangled me day and night. I remained alone in my room and wailed for days. No food went to my mouth and my eyes lacked sleep. The blow was too intense which knocked me down completely. My heart was ripped apart. I couldn't forget that gruesome image of mom lying lifelessly in the blood pool. Her thoughts kept burning me alive and I could not bear them anymore. To get rid of these thoughts and to attain some relief from this anguish, I decided to do one thing....

Straight away, I reached dad's room and opened the door hesitantly. In the dimness of the bed light, I saw dad in deep sleep. He was not at all aware of my presence and kept snoring. Keeping an eye on dad, I slowly walked towards the cupboard and opened it gently without imposing any sound. From that cupboard, I picked a heroin pack and got out of the room in the same secrecy.

Getting back to my room, I stripped open that pack and put some of the heroin powder on the table. I rolled up a banknote and snorted that powder through it. After a moment, I felt eased and some kind of happiness kicked in me. Suddenly, I started crying. I didn't understand why I was crying? Maybe it was because of my mom's death, or maybe due to that high happiness! My mind felt completely clouded! At the same time, I felt extremely drowsy. . . 'For the first time since mom's death, my eyes felt sleepy'. . . Bluety's actions and swaying pendulum in the wall clock seemed to be slowed down in that drowsy state. Staring at that pendulum, I fell flat on the bed and my eyes slowly closed.

I sensed a furious voice shouting to wake me up, along with continuous patting on my shoulder. Sensing this rampage, my eyes opened slowly and I saw dad beside me. His face looked infuriated. In a drowsy state, I woke up and sat on the bed by looking dad's furious face.

Dad threw a newspaper at me. When I picked that newspaper into my hands, I saw my picture from last night while snorting heroin, with the headline 'Little legend is a druggie'.

'Fuck! How did it come out?' I was shocked while seeing that newspaper.

'Is this real...?' Dad asked in rage.

I remained silent with my head down.

'Have you done this? Speak out dammit,' dad's tone raised high.

'Yes....' I nodded.

As soon as I gestured this, dad slapped me.

'How do you know this...?' shouted dad.

'I saw you many times while taking this,' I replied in an apologizing tone.

'Idiot, what's the necessity to take this?'

'What to do! When mom's thoughts were crucifying me every second.' I said and burst out in tears.

With my outburst, dad's face turned pity. He said nothing but consoled me by gripping my shoulder.

'I'm sorry....' Dad said in a sympathetic tone.   'Do you still have it with you?' He asked about heroin.

'No....' I lied.

I lied because I felt it could keep me away from this agonizing distress.

'Good. Don't even try to take it again. And, if anyone questions you about this, tell them that the image was morphed.' Saying this, dad walked off the room.

After his exit, I picked that heroin pack from the table and hidden it deep under the mattress.

I never stopped taking heroin secretly. In the time of this great distress, having it felt so good and relieved. I even started consuming alcohol to keep my mind away from mom's tragedy. While having alcohol, my endearment on mom came out as a song. Suppressing the grief within me, I wrote that song to make a Single as a tribute to mom by releasing it on her birthday which was about to come in next month. Lyrics of the song seemed heart touchingly beautiful, and I expected it to be a gem of a Single.

While I was planning to make this song a standout one, media once again released my private stuff. This time it was the videos revealing me drinking alcohol and snorting heroin. I was absolutely outraged and had no clue how and who shot these videos!

'It happened exactly as I feared.... Previously, fame had followed me whenever I was out. But now the legendary status brought intrusions even into my bedroom, revealing the confidential matters of my private life. Can my life ever be in my control from now or will legendary status completely annihilate me?' I worried.

News channels started to create fuss on these leaked videos and characterized me as a spoiled brat. World does not see anything profoundly. Nobody cared about my suffering and the reason behind taking the drugs. Media always needed some stuff to assail me and they got what they wanted. Media's overreaction on this matter hurt me. And an excessive hatred had formed in me towards the media.

In the time of this oppressed attack from the media, I went to the studio to make mom's song. After recording the song, I came out of studio to go home. But then, in front of that studio, a large number of reporters encircled me while I was walking towards my car.

'Edward, Edward, Edward... What is your stance on those leaked videos? Are you admitting your mistake? What's your reply to the people who were blaming your parents for your misconduct?' Reporters accosted me with these queries.

Their questions exasperated me. I was not able to digest the criticism on my parents and the media's mess with my personal life. Immediately, my fury flared up.

'Who the hell are you people to intervene in my private life. Bloody disgusting ass holes,' I burst out on the reporters and smashed their cameras.

With my act, media provoked a storm against me and roasted me heavily. I was quite devastated by this charge from the media. During this undesired period of turmoil, another blow struck me hard....

The song that I was making for mom had been leaked to the web even before composing music. Some anti-forces that intended to do me harm leaked the song. Obviously, song was patchy as it was under construction and bland without any music. My desire of paying a grand tribute to mom and hope that this song will be a top-notch work of mine was ruined with this leak. It was quite a hard blow and I was absolutely shattered. Suddenly, an insecure feeling broke out in me with all these leaks. It felt like I was left alone in the battle field against this fucking world. . .   'How good it would be if my mom was here with me now! She could be a great support for me during this sad plight,' suffering the painful time alone, I cried my heart out. . .

I grew more anxious with all the undesired incidents that were happening around me. To calm down my nerves from this disturbing situation, I opened a whiskey bottle. While having whiskey, my room's door opened, and Rosie, a subordinate, entered with dinner. Her face was left in shock at seeing whiskey glass in my mouth. Suddenly, a panic kicked in me at her unexpected arrival.

'Why did you come in! Did I ask for dinner?' I shouted at her, hiding the whiskey glass to my side.

'No. But… but your father called me and asked to give this to you...' She said, tensed.

'Keep it there, and get out from here.'

She kept the dinner plate on the table and left the room. Immediately after her exit, I got suspicious of her. . . 'Shit! Did she secretly take my footage while I was having alcohol???'. . . With this doubt, I rushed to the door and called her into my room. Once she stepped in, my hands went through her earrings and shirt buttons in search for any tiny camera. She expressed embarrassment while my hands ran through her. But I didn't stop my search. After going through the buttons, I put my hand in her breast pocket.

'No.... Edward, what are you doing!' She shouted, mortified as she covered her breasts with her arms.

But ignoring her, I continued to search that pocket button over her breast. While I was doing this, she pushed my hand away and ran out of the room, weeping. Although I did not find any camera with her, I did not feel sorry for her. Well, after all the disturbing incidents that had happened in my life recently, all I cared about was to protect my private data. I did not allow myself to feel bad for others.

With her exit, I locked the door. I now began to suspect that Rosie or other staff who had previously entered my room might have kept a hidden camera. So I searched every object in my room for any hidden cameras. But I couldn't even find one. I then sat down to have whiskey. But still, an insecure feeling kept running through my mind, suggesting that someone was observing me in secrecy. With this suspicion, I turned off the lights in my room. The darkness around felt so safe because no one could stalk me or even get a glimpse of me in this dark. Feeling secure in that darkness, I continued to drink whiskey.

With all those leaks, I started to look at the world with skepticism. I kept an investigative eye on every person around me in the mansion because I failed to locate the source from where the leaks had happened! Subordinates who entered my room seemed suspicious to me as if they were trying to steal some private data of mine. I felt insecure from all corners. Fearing that the subordinates might bring some difficulties, I did not allow them to enter my room anymore. Only Aston was permitted in to tend to my needs. For fear of people spying over me, I continued to live in the darkness of my room. No sunlight entered my room through the black window curtains. Even the lights that I turned off in my room were never put on again because of this fear. No, it was not fear anymore. I must say, it had turned into a phobia. . . 'A phobia of people and light'. . . Because of this phobia, I refused to face people and to be in any part of light. Anyone close to me felt like an intrusion and any light around was a suffocation. I even kept myself away from studios without attending to recordings.

On one side, there was the torment of my mom's death, on the other side, my phobia had started to fill depressing thoughts in me. I constantly felt panic and hopelessness. I was completely in despair and broken. All the awful incidents that had happened recently left an incurable wound in my heart and it kept on bleeding. Unable to tolerate this painful tribulation, I got addicted to drugs and alcohol.

To bring me out from this depressed state, dad assigned counselling therapies with a renowned psychiatrist Dr David Jones, a good friend of dad. I was absolutely scared and reluctant to attend those therapies. But I was dragged to his office anyhow....

Even at the psychiatrist's office, people did not afford me any calm. The place where every person's mental scar reduces, generated even more agony for me with staff and people's overwhelming reception. I was utterly terrified by this and stayed silent with my head down. After five minutes of chaos, dad's private security took over control of the situation.

Leaving me, Justin Langer and his security back in the lobby, dad went to meet the psychiatrist in person. There were about 20 people around me in that lobby. By seeing all the illuminating lights in that lobby along with those people's voracious looks towards me had increased my terror. I noticed that I was being papped by a couple of people who were waiting alongside in that lobby. By witnessing this atrocious environment around me, panic kicked inside me. Right away, I feared impending doom and my body started shivering. My heart pounded violently. I couldn't breathe properly and some sort of tightness strangled my throat. Even in that air conditioning lobby, sweat oozed out heavily from my skin pores. The bright lights kept terrorizing me and I couldn't tolerate those humans around. I felt like a fawn surrounded by a ferocious pride. I could not hang in there anymore and my horrified mind urged me to run away from there. Immediately, I stood up and started walking without looking at anyone around there.

'Where are you going?' Justin Langer questioned me from behind.

I didn't even turn around, but kept walking forward by raising my little finger, gesturing nature's call. Slowly moving towards the toilet, I picked up pace at once and sprinted outwards without getting into the toilet. I didn't even look back whether Justin and security were chasing me or not!

Running out of that building, I saw our car at the parking slot with chauffeur inside it. Straight away, I reached there and threw him out of the car. Getting into the driving seat, I started the engine and fled away from there....

I knew that dad would be incensed at me for running away, and would definitely pull me to that psychiatrist's office again if I went home. So, I did not drive the car towards home. I didn't even know where I was going. I just kept stepping hard on the accelerator to flee as far as possible from this world. With the constant presence of people and traffic around my car, I kept finding vacant roads. This took me to Epping Forest after 50 minutes of blistering drive. I didn't imagine I would end up in this forest. Reaching here was not deliberate but purely accidental. The place seemed so isolated with woodlands occupying in all directions. There was a narrow road passing through the middle of that woodland, on which there were no other vehicles. I could not see a single human there. It felt like time had given me a golden opportunity to live away from people and I decided to grab it with both hands. Immediately, I stopped my car at the roadside and got down. Sensing the seclusion of that forest and twilight sky above, an intense high grabbed me. I walked into the forest with an insane cry.

Stepping far from people made me relieved. I was not at all interested in seeing any faces or getting out of this forest. I ate what I got. It felt so good having some food in the middle of the forest 'miles away from the world'. Even the sumptuous meals prepared by the chefs at the mansion never brought this much delight to my heart. In the remoteness of that forest, sleeping on the dry muddy surface and counting the stars over my head during nights was a sublime experience. In the mornings, I saw birds flying in the skies. I kept listening to their melodious chirps throughout the day. With all these, it felt so good to be in the forest than in the world. There were no barriers for me now and I did what I wanted. I played with little animals by chasing them. I plucked the fruits. I swam in the nearby water bodies. This exile gave me a tiny bit of relief from mom's tragedy and all the mess that happened in recent times.

I sustained 4 days in that forest. Thereafter, unable to get enough food, I became very weak. But even then, I never thought of going back. After some time, I saw troops searching for me. Not at all willing to step back into the vicious world, I kept evading them. . . 'How did they know I was here? Well, I got the answer instantly. They might have known I was here because of the car I left in the woods'. . .

A day later, the remaining energy in me was completely gone. There was no strength left in my body. I could not move even an inch and collapsed to the ground. I then lost consciousness....

I opened my eyes back at home and came to know that I was rescued by those troops after losing consciousness. At this moment, the only thought that ran in my mind was, 'How nice it would have been, if I had died in that forest!' But time didn't let it happen.

My life was completely ruined and it could never be healed. Perceiving the hurting fact that there will be no joy and freedom for me any further, I sketched a bird with broken wings on my chest in anguish. But my insanity didn't stop with a temporary sketch and I cried out for a permanent one, because I knew that this torment would last till I drew my last breath. So, I turned that temporary sketch into a permanent tattoo.

Nothing seemed to have changed in my life after returning back. It's the same devastation and distress. It's the same suspicion and fear. I locked myself in the room and didn't even step out, because I had already found a safe heaven in the darkness of my room. Dad pleaded with me to come out by promising that he will never take me to counselling therapies again. But I ignored dad's pleas and constrained myself within the darkness of my room.

Due to my misery, dad was stuck in a dilemma whether to continue or withdraw me from my ongoing music commitments. Then, I myself found a way. To relieve this terrible distress, I spent a considerable amount of time composing music behind the closed doors of my room. Noticing this passion of mine towards music, dad came up with a new idea....

He constructed an own private studio for me in the premises of our house, which grants me complete privacy from the world. Maybe, his intention was to make me continue my music, so that his music company can gain profits from me. Whatever the reason could be, I got a secure place to work on music. No one was permitted to enter that studio, apart from very few of my beloved technicians who committed to work for my albums.

Far away from the public eye, inside the dark chambers of my private studio, I kept working on my music. Grasping my undying love of music, dad's shattered hopes came alive. He continued to produce my albums and never stopped making money from them.

As time passed on, I didn't show any willingness to step out of the estate because I had found my pleasant and secure workplace at the premises of home itself. Thus, I restricted myself only to the estate. Any recordings of mine used to take place only at nights in my studio. In fear that some anti forces might infiltrate, I started using a customized wrist watch. This watch was designed to let me know about the presence of any new people around by tracing their mobile signals. If the watch detects any signal, it will sound a beeping alert.

One night, while in deep sleep, I recalled the most precious moment of my life. In fact, it was the only happy time in my entire life. This moment was from my early years when I was tiny. Those were the days, when the world don't know about me and I probably lived without any concern of stardom. It was a delightful moment like never before, and my distressing life didn't gave any chance to be happy thereafter. I can never forget that great feeling of happiness. I can never forget my delightful laughs of that time.

My happiest moment

'A lovely evening. Somewhere in the breathtakingly beautiful farms surrounded with high raised fjords. I saw a few butterflies fluttering its wings and flying all around in the garden in front of a wooden house. In that place, my nose could sense a sweet fragrance. I didn't know where that fragrance was coming from? But I was so enthralled and my mood enhanced because of inhaling that fragrance. By seeing those butterflies and experiencing such a lovely environment around, an instant happiness kicked in. Immediately, I started chasing those butterflies in great happiness and laughed while inhaling that sweet fragrance. Flying away from me, a butterfly landed on the plant and hid behind its leaves. I raised my little hand to catch it. But even before my hand reached that butterfly, it flew and landed on my wrist. Seeing that exquisite butterfly on my wrist, my heart danced in delight. My little brain felt that butterfly liked me so much and that's why it had perched on me. I gently took that butterfly to my lips and kissed it. As soon as I did this, it flew away from me by fluttering its beautiful wings. I did nothing to catch that butterfly again, but simply kept staring at it with great content'......... When my mind was totally overwhelmed by this great pleasure, my ear suddenly heard the alarm ring. Thus, I woke up at once. As soon as I woke up, all I could see around me was the pitch darkness of my room. In that dead darkness, the ringing alarm clock on the bed side table indicated 7:30 P.M. It's a recording night for me. . . 'Damn! How bad was the time! It doesn't even want me to enjoy the dearest memory of my life for some more while,' I scolded the time within me and got up from the bed to get ready for my recording. . .

After getting dressed up in my dressing room, I heard a sudden thud of an object from outside. Following this sound, my ears caught the low voices of two people. Immediately, a doubt arose in me that someone was spying on me from outside! Quickly, I rushed towards that dressing room's window to get a clear picture of what was going outside! There, around that dressing room's window, I noticed a few tiny objects were strewn and also the curtain was fluttering due to wind from outside because the window was opened. Hiding behind that fluttering curtain, I peeped out through that window. In the soft glow of outside light, I noticed a trail of shoe prints in snow. Those shoe prints were pointing out from the house towards the hedge.

'Fuck.... Someone invaded my room and escaped by jumping out of this window.' I thought in fright by seeing those shoe prints.

Strewn objects around and the opened window of the dressing room added strength to my fear. Alarmed that there had been an intrusion, I dashed out of the mansion to catch the intruder. Under the night snowing sky, I started following those shoe prints in panic. Suddenly, my wrist watch started to sound a beeping alert. Immediately, a terror kicked in me. I turned off the alert and hid in the hedge which was to my side. Putting step by step towards the left (where those shoe prints trails), I reached the corner of that hedge. From that corner, I peeped to see where those shoe prints were heading. The trail of shoe prints ended up at the estate's compound wall, where I saw a few workmen working over the broken part of that wall. At this moment, one of the workmen who was puffing a cigarette near that hedge spotted me.

'Oh my God... Edward!!!' He said this with an astounded face as he dropped the cigarette.

Some kind of enthusiasm was literally dancing inside him and I could clearly sense it in his face.

'Hey guys look here... Here's Edward Bell,' he shouted frantically towards his colleagues who were working on the broken wall in the distance.

Turning the work lights towards us, all the workmen over there stared intensely at me. When they started to advance towards me, I was absolutely horrified and thumbed the button of my watch, alerting mansion's security. Within few seconds, security reached me.

'Some of these buggers invaded my room and stole my data. Nab them and get it back,' I ordered the security in a trembling voice.

Safeguarding me from those workmen, security brought me back to my room.

A short while after the incident, I was comforted by dad who sat alongside me in my room.

'Has the security found the intruder?' I asked dad in worry.

Blowing air out of his nose in vexation, dad replied in a pitiful tone, 'We checked CCTV footage, no one entered your room Joe.'

'No dad, they invaded me. I saw a trail of shoe prints from the house towards the compound wall.'

'Those shoe prints may belong to workmen who came to store some equipment in the storeroom beneath your room. They did not enter your room. Trust me, I myself checked the CCTV footage. It's only your fear, which is causing anxiety and making you assume that they invaded you. But in reality, no such thing had happened,' explained dad.

I was not at all convinced by what dad said!

'No. You are hiding something from me. If they had not invaded me, why was the dressing room's window open and objects around it strewn?' I questioned.

Frustrated, dad showed me the footage recorded by the CCTV camera installed at the lawn, which monitors my room from outside. This footage revealed that the dressing room's window was opened by Aston while cleaning the room in the morning and never closed thereafter.

'Now you got it... Aston may have forgot to close the window, and outside wind made the curtain to flutter. This fluttering curtain may have disturbed the objects near that window,' dad said.

After watching that footage and listening to dad's words, I said nothing. But still, doubts didn't leave my mind. I strongly kept believing that something had happened against me!!!

My fear of intrusion kept getting worse each day. I made a habit of suspecting my own surroundings and kept thinking there was a conspiracy against me. But shockingly, none of these suspicions eventually proved to be true. As a result of all these stressful incidents, doctor prescribed medications to relieve my anxiety. Gah! My stardom finally made me a mentally ill person and put me on meds.

ADULTHOOD - (NAIL IN THE COFFIN)

17 years later

My anxiety never saw an end since the past 17 years and it kept reversing again and again once the prescribed course of medication was finished. I was advised many types of medications in these years, from Paroxetine to Sertraline, from Clonazepam to Alprazolam. But nothing kept my anxiety permanently away. Still, to this date, it's the same fear towards people, and it's the same suspicion upon the world.

Due to the fear of people, I had locked myself in the darkness of my private space for all these years, completely detached from the world. This in turn had affected my creativity in composing songs, because my loneliness and phobia didn't give me an opportunity to find new experiences in life. All the albums I have done recently are inspired from my old tunes. I simply changed the formula of those old tunes and made them into new ones. Because of this, these recent albums seemed like old wine in new bottles. Even my sense of mood had shown a strong impact in my recent albums. Lyrics in these songs represented my state of mind which was consumed with distress. Though the majority of these albums became successful in the market, I was so upset that I was unable to make new kinds of songs like I did in the past years.

If I keep music aside for a moment and look into my life, nothing has changed within me. But, many things have changed around me drastically in these 17 years.... Dad married another woman. She was not a middle class woman like mom. She was from one of the richest families of Wales. Dad was happy because she was business minded like him. They both together expanded the business empire to great heights. My grandpa (William Bell) who was an idol and a mentor during the initial stage of my music career had passed away recently. Even Bluety departed this life 13 years ago, leaving me alone. In this loneliness, the sole person I could find around was Aston. Other than him, I had lost everyone whom I adored.

After all these years of bumpy life, another hard blow tore me apart. This blow was a sheer brutal one which almost made me draw my last breath....

That mayhem began at night in my private studio. After completing the recording, I went to my private room and started taking whiskey. Suddenly, under the faint sodium lamp glow in that room, I saw the almirah door was slightly opened. Panic arose in me as I started to think why and who opened that almirah? Pondering this, I got up from the couch by placing whiskey glass on the table to my front and walked to that almirah. Once I pulled that half opened almirah door, I saw that the locker inside it was also opened. My panic increased exponentially. I quickly looked into that locker and came to know that a bag in which a few hard drives containing my ongoing album data had been missing from it. Deducing that infiltration had happened, I slammed the almirah door in fury.

To find the intruder, I switched on the monitor in my room. CCTV footage from the corridor showed a person fleeing with my stolen bag. I was outraged upon seeing this. Immediately, I raised the alarm to alert our security. I picked up my gun from the drawer and rushed to the corridor to nab that intruder. Reaching the corridor, I saw him fleeing towards the steps of the corridor.

'Stop there you mother fucker....' I shouted in fury while chasing him.

Completely ignoring me, he exited the corridor and ran downstairs. I followed him downstairs. On reaching the ground floor, I saw that intruder jumping out from the window. He might have done this to escape from the security officers who were approaching him from the other end. I reached that window and saw him attacking my chief security officer who came there to catch him. He then pushed the chief security officer away and climbed the compound wall of the studio to jump to the other side. Unable to stop him from fleeing away, I totally went out of control and fired the shot at him. The bullet hit him in the back and he fell backwards in excruciating pain. As he was lying on the ground far from me, I wasn't able to identify who he was! Our security officers rushed at him and detained him. When I reached that intruder to collect my stolen bag, I identified him. He's a person who was recently recruited in the maintenance department of my studio. Security officers recovered the stolen bag from him and further searched all his body. Then, they found a spy pen camera in his pocket and a wallet. When I opened that wallet, I saw his freelance journalist Id card in it. With this, it became clear for me about his background and his intention behind this intrusion. Security officers took him to hospital.

I connected that pen camera to the computer. The footage captured by that journalist was mind boggling. He captured every corner, chamber, and security details of my studio. He even filmed me and Aston secretly while we were discussing about the heroin package which was supposed to arrive at midnight. . . . 'Oh my god. What if the footage in this device has gone out???' I thought to myself, worried. . . . I destroyed that pen camera and its footage by burning it.

A while later.... When contemplating the incident, guilt had swelled in me for wounding a person. I deeply regretted my act towards that person. I felt so sorry for him. Alongside this remorse, a fear started to build in me about the consequences of shooting a journalist.

When I was repenting for what I've done, media broke the news that I shot a journalist. News channels portrayed me as a brute, completely ignoring the robbery done by that journalist. I was heartbroken because of this.

Police came to the studio for investigation upon the statement given by that injured journalist who mentioned that I shot him for secretly filming the conversation about the drugs. I was outraged as the journalist hid his robbery and stated that I shot him for filming the conversation about the drugs. . . "Grr! Because of my wrongful act, for the first time in my life I felt sorry for an unknown person. But what has that person done to me instead? He didn't even regret his act and simply blamed me as if he had made no mistake. Because of this, my remorse had evaporated on that journalist". . . Police questioned me regarding the shooting. I stated to the police that I had nothing to do with the shooting and it was him who robbed my bag containing hard drives and escaped. Police checked the CCTV footage. The footage from the corridor showed the journalist running away with my stolen bag and I chasing him with a gun in my hand. Police came to the conclusion that I had shot the journalist by seeing this footage showing me chasing him with a gun. They seized my gun and sent it for forensic examination. With the statement given by that injured journalist and with the evidence of the CCTV footage from the corridor, police arrested me and took me to the station. After many years, this was the first time for me to step out of the estate premises and I was so scared.

Later, police took me to the court. I was extremely scared by seeing the people at the court. I wasn't able to get a grip on myself and fell into an extreme tizzy due to the presence of those people. Aston came to the court along with my lawyer. Seeing Aston, I felt a bit relieved. My lawyer took care of the legal formalities in the court.

I was produced in front of a judge. Court clerk read the charge filed against me and asked me to plead guilty or not guilty. I pleaded not guilty to avoid the immediate sentence. The case proceeded to trial and I was given bail.

While I was stepping out of the court, I saw a group of journalists protesting against me for shooting the journalist. I was so scared at seeing them and stopped at the entrance of the court. My heart suggested not to care about those dogs and to get away from there quickly. Following this advice, I moved forward by mustering up the courage. Suddenly, I noticed a shoe coming towards my head swiftly from those protesters. I didn't know which person in the protesters had thrown it? As an immediate reaction, I stopped walking and hid my face behind my palms. But the shoe breached through my palms and hit my forehead. I was in shock, holding my bleeding forehead. Though my wound was bleeding, the pain didn't hurt me much, because this insult had caused intense pain to me inwardly, overshadowing the physical pain. I swayed in fury with this humiliating incident. Right away, I surged towards the protesters.

'No Joe, control yourself. Look, media is covering this. Please don't create a scene here,' said Aston, stopping me.

If Aston had not stopped me, it would have turned into another catastrophic event. Holding my fury within me, I got into the car and left the place.

Journalists started the protests in front of my estate. On the other hand, fake news began to circulate in the social-media that the journalist came to the studio for my interview and saw me taking drugs and filmed me secretly, and I noticed this and shot him in uncontrollable anger. I was utterly infuriated by this slander. Believing this fake news, common people had also joined the journalists' protests and completely besieged the estate. Because of these ghastly protests, I had grown more anxious. I wasn't able to withstand this gruesome situation and surrendered to it wholly. I was mentally collapsed. I was so dreaded. There was no courage left in me to fight this situation.

Though I dropped my bundle, dad didn't. He started to turn things in favour of me to bring me out from this case. Dad offered a huge sum of money to the studio's chief security officer and asked him to confess that he shot the journalist. He agreed to this. Dad along with my lawyer made up a story that when the journalist was escaping with my stolen bag, chief security officer caught him, then the Journalist attacked the officer and for the sake of self defence he shot the journalist. The chief security officer was asked to tell this to the court. Dad bribed the police and asked them to make a report that the fired bullet came from the studio's chief security officer's gun. To counter the video evidence from the corridor, my lawyer planned to tell the court that I chased the journalist with a gun just to threaten him not to run away but didn't shoot him. With these moves, dad was confident that I will get rid of this case.

The day had come for me to attend the court for trial. I was stuck in absolute terror as I must step out into the atrocious world and face the court. "Can I deal with the court? Can I deal with the people? That day, someone threw a shoe at me, now will the same be repeated or will I go through something even worse? Although if I somehow escape from the people, do I have the guts to face the court? What was going to happen in court? Am I going to face more troubles there? In case I face unexpected troubles, will I succumb to them? Oh no, how to overcome this grievous crisis???" These disturbing thoughts occupied my mind.

I tried so hard to get rid of these frightening thoughts but couldn't. Tension increased severely in me and I was unable to bear it anymore. To calm my nerves, I took an Alprazolam pill and got ready to attend court. But one single pill didn't show any effect and my anxiety kept on rising without an end. Unable to withstand this intense anxiety, I opened the Alprazolam bottle and poured some more pills into my palm. I put those pills in my mouth and gulped a glass of neat whiskey. I thought taking these pills in high doses in combination with alcohol would give an instant calming effect to my panicking mind, so that I can get some courage to face the world. Then, I left for court.

While I was on the way to court, something strange began to happen in my body. It became difficult for me to breathe. A kind of drowsiness struck me. My muscles turned weak. I could clearly sense an abnormality in my heartbeat and I experienced dragging pain in my chest. Alongside this pain, severe headache and dizziness started to trouble me. My whole body began to quiver. My vision turned blurry and trippy. When I looked to my front, the chauffeur who was riding the car and Aston who was sitting next to him, appeared in doubled and tripled vision. Even passing vehicles on the road looked the same.

In such a terrible situation, I reached the court and went inside along with Aston and my lawyer. I didn't know how I managed to walk in such a weakened state! But I did. Every object and person in the court appeared in the same tripped vision. Though I could see people around me, I did not feel so frightened. Maybe, it could be the effect of those pills I took!

A few minutes later, I was called into the courtroom. Usher showed me the way to the defendant dock and I took my seat in that dock in the same weakened state. But then, my condition worsened. My eyes weren't able to get any clear picture over the surroundings and turned more blurry. Dizziness reached to the extreme and I lost control over my body and collapsed in the dock. I saw a few people rushing towards me in the same blurred vision. Then, my eyes went closed....

When I opened my eyes, what I could sense in my hazy vision was the ICU environment. I could vaguely see doctors examining me, but I was unable to react or respond to anything. Sensing the doctors and the scary environment around, a kind of confusion and agitation struck me. My brain was unable to understand what was going on! I wasn't able to move.

As the time passed on, I felt some improvement in my condition. Unlike previously, now I was able to move my upper and lower limbs and respond to the doctors. But the presence of the doctors worried me a lot. Though I felt to run away from them, my body did not cooperate to do so and I stuck to the bed. I was asked my date of birth, father's birthplace, current and past three Prime Ministers? I answered each question with a lack of strength in my voice, feeling weak. Then I was asked about the events I remembered before going unconscious, and the events I remembered since I opened my eyes in the hospital? As I remembered these, I explained what had happened. I didn't understand why the doctor was asking me all these! Then the doctor said that I came out of coma after 6 weeks and to examine my memory he was asking me these. It felt like the bottom had dropped out of my stomach after listening to what the doctor said. I was shocked. I was lost for words. When I was thinking of how I went into a coma, I was told that this happened due to the drug overdose. Doctor said that I was doing well and there was no need to worry. After performing some checkups, doctors exited the room.

With the exit of the doctors, dad entered. He seemed heartbroken. Plummeting on a stool which was next to my bed, dad took my palm into his hands and broke down into tears. I didn't expect such an emotional reaction from dad. His face, which was always lit with high confidence and pride, seemed so peculiar in this distressing mood. Dad didn't say anything for a moment. Then, he broke the silence in the same devastating tears, 'Are you mad! Will anyone take depressant drug in such a high dose, that too mixed with alcohol'.

'I thought taking them could give me the strength to face the people and the court,' I replied in a weak tone.

'You may have thought so. But actually, you almost dug your own grave stupid. Doctors said that your brain was severely affected and chances of your recovery was low. But luckily, you have recovered.'

'I didn't expect this to happen dad,' I said while feeling sorry for myself.

'Your mom often used to argue with me for continuing you in music. Maybe she had anticipated this kind of disaster. If I had listened to her then, your life would have been so different today. Directly or indirectly, I'm the reason for what has happened to you. I'm sorry Joe.' Dad said in remorse.

For the first time in my life, I saw dad regretting his decision. He also seemed very affectionate towards me now in contrast to the past. Definitely, these changes could be the result of a father's anguish by seeing his son fighting for life for weeks.

'Anyway, it's great to have you back Joe. Have some rest for now, I will see you soon,' dad said, patting my hand and getting up from the stool.

When he was walking away from me towards the exit, I called him. With my call, dad turned back at me.

'How is that journalist now?' I asked.

'He's fine.' Dad replied.

'What about the case?' I asked.

'Your lawyer represented you in the court and stated that you chased the journalist with a gun just to threaten him not to run away and you have nothing to do with the shooting, and the footage of you chasing him with a gun will not attest that you shot him. Police submitted a report that the fired bullet came from the studio's chief security officer's gun. The chief security officer confessed that he shot the journalist in self-defence. I made a compromise with that journalist and he told the court that he mistakenly assumed that you shot him due to the presence of the gun in your hand. Court declared you innocent. There's no need to worry anymore. Keep your mind peaceful and take rest.' Saying this, dad opened the door and went out of the room.

'Oh! Eventually my phobia had pushed me to the brink of death. Am I lucky to cheat death? Or is this a warning bell suggesting that what had happened till now was enough, and somehow find a way to get away from all the fears.' My mind was filled with these thoughts after knowing what my fears had done to me. I couldn't get rid of these thoughts whatsoever.

A few days later, I was shifted to home. A doctor and a nurse were designated to take care of me at home.... Though I escaped death, the dreadful feeling of having almost perished kept haunting me. I constantly worried about what would happen to me in future if my fears kept continuing like this! I felt my fears would definitely see my end if I couldn't find a way to get away from them immediately. With this concern, I kept on thinking how I could find a permanent solution to my fears? After numerous thoughts, finally I got an idea which could keep me away from all my fears and abate my distress....

That idea was to quit my music career and to move far away from this awful world. I felt that if I still continued my career, my ever-growing popularity, constant attention from the media, fans and the society would only worsen my fears and the condition of my mental health. In addition to this, when I looked back into my life, I failed to find even one good day in which I lived peacefully after becoming a celebrity. After going through all those painful years, I realized I could never live serenely with my celebrity status. Thus I thought if I terminate my career and move far away from the public eye, I could put an end to my fame and I could live my life as I desire. With this intent, I decided to start a new life as a new person far away from this world.

After completely recovering, I said my decision to dad. I thought he would oppose me. But he didn't and vowed to give me his full support. I felt happy to see the change in dad.

I scouted for a perfect hideaway across the UK, but failed to find a desired asset which would grant me total privacy from the people. After a few more attempts, I finally discovered a small hilly island which seemed as a perfect place for seeking complete solitude. This island was located about 2 miles away from the mid coast of Norway in the Atlantic Ocean. Facing eastward, the isle is located in the Norwegian sea, and surrounded by tall mountains in the ocean on its either side. Not only providing seclusion from the people, this island has another distinguishing characteristic which attracted me a lot. . . 'Nature's music such as whispering winds, waves sounds and birds chirps could be heard in every corner of the island at every time, somewhat resembling my 'Edwardzee' style of music. Because of this, every second on this island felt like I was living with music. I thought that this nature's music around the island will also help to ease up my distressed state of mind'. . . I was so excited to find this kind of place in mom's home country, in which I was also born.

Within 12 months, that hilly island was transformed into a new mode as per my requirement. I named this island after my mom as 'Elin Oakrill'. The island was equipped with lavish lawns, beautiful gardens, golf course, cricket pitch and fountains. Main building on the island was built to look the same as my house in London. Even the interiors of this main building were designed exactly like London's house. The reason for me to construct the island's main building in this way was to replicate my house in London, so that it would give me a feeling of living in my old home in which I lived all my life. To spend some time with my feathered friends, a nest house was built upon an oak tree which contained a bird colony.

Once all the construction work on the island was completed, I permanently shifted to Norway in secrecy to start my new life. The only person who came with me to Norway was Aston. He took care of all my needs on the island.

Alongside taking care of my needs, another responsibility was given to Aston by dad. As I was reluctant to use mobile phone fearing that I may get tapped, dad had no scope to know any information about me. So, Aston was assigned to inform dad about every change, positive or negative, that happens to me.... Keeping in tune with my mood, dad developed a peculiar routine. Every once in a while, an object of my liking had arrived at the island along with a letter of advice from dad. First he sent me the world's most expensive champagne. Dad intended for me to open this bottle as a sign of celebration for starting a new life. 'Humm, celebration! Except for pain and agony, what I was left with to celebrate?' I thought to myself and kept that bottle aside without opening.

After this champagne bottle, dad kept sending me hypercars one after another. By sending these cars, dad might have thought that I would step out from the island to roam in these as I love driving. But I did not drive any of these cars and locked them in the coast building's cellar, because I felt these cars would gain a lot of attention from the people if spotted on the road.

While I'm getting used to this new life, two of my albums which I made just before going to coma had been released by dad. Upon my plan, dad did this purposefully to mislead the people that I'm still living in London and working on my albums after coming out from coma. I wanted the people to believe that I'm living in London, so that I can live peacefully in Norway without any troubles.

After the release of these two albums, no album of mine hit the market. This poor world kept on waiting for the release of my new albums. But the fact that the world doesn't know was, I had already withdrawn my career and relocated to my island.

ADULTHOOD - (CHANGED TIMES)

2 Years Later

I grew a long beard and hair with the intention of erasing my identity. Even my clothes were designed to be loose to keep my body shape hidden. As I love black, I stuck to black tone clothing. I made a habit of using black Hoodie to cover my face whenever I was out of my island. This black coloured clothing helped me to merge with the darkness. With this transformation, I wanted all the traces of my past to be completely wiped out.

My life on the island seemed so different when compared to my life in London. There were no worries about the presence of people around me now. Most of my days on the island passed well. I enjoyed my solitude by regularly having Myken whiskey in pair with my favourite Duffy's chocolates. I carried on with my hobbies such as reading books, writing poetry, playing golf, and learning new techniques in extracting fragrances from the flowers and shrubs. Other activities like watching birds flying, and spending time in serene landscapes of my island, provided a little solace during the inactive day.

I often used to go out at midnights to enjoy driving on the vacant roads and to gather some aromatic flowers and shrubs at the nearby isolated fjords. During these times, instead of going in the hypercars, I used Volkswagen Golf to maintain the low profile. I chose this car because it has an engaging driving experience in budget cars.

Although I had quit my music career, I continued to compose songs in solitude to satisfy my zeal. But I never intended these songs to be released to the public. Along with composing music, I also followed my passion for painting. Throughout the years, my music went to every corner of the world. But painting remained very personal and close to my heart as I expressed my feelings to myself.

Since I shifted to Norway, I have made many paintings portraying the concealed emotions of my heart. In all these paintings, I continued with my signature style of inducing senses such as smell and sounds into my paintings according to the mood of that portrayal.

With the successful outcome of these paintings, it was time for me to portray the most precious artwork of my life.... There was only one happy time in my entire life in which I remembered my joyfulness and laughs while chasing butterflies in a beautiful farm. This incident was from my childhood before obtaining stardom. As my whole life was ruined in pain and misery, this childhood memory showed me the aspect of joy. I can see that memory in my mind as my point of view. Which means, I cannot see my laughs and happiness combined with my joyful face. So, the purest emotion of my memory which had existed only in my heart needed to be transferred into my childhood face via painting. Unlike my previous paintings, this painting was completely different because I have to portray a joyful face which I had never successfully done before. So instead of working directly on painting, I firstly made a sketch. I utterly failed in matching the intensity of my laughs and happiness of my memory in that sketch. As days went by, I made several sketches for my painting but couldn't capture the true joy behind the laughs and happiness of my memory. Unwilling to give up, I kept on sketching my childhood face repeatedly.

The other accurate thing from my past memory which had stored in my mind was, an alluring sweet fragrance which spread all over that locale while I was chasing those butterflies. Remembering my pleasant mood while experiencing that fragrance, I concluded that this smell would define my mood in the painting. More importantly, I felt that fragrance was one of the major elements which enhanced my joyfulness even more at the time of my memory. So, I decided to blend this fragrance as the smell of the background location in my painting. By blending this smell into the painting, my intention was to capture my mood at the time of my memory. But I couldn't remember the exact source of that fragrance which filled up that location. As I was unable to remember from where that smell came from, my frustration grew exponentially with time.

One day, I carried on sketching my childhood face again and again but failed in capturing the true joy of my memory. I was outraged with my failure. Suddenly, the serene ambience of my art room was broken by the clamour of sketch papers flying all around, clattering paint jars and snapping wooden easels as I smashed these objects altogether and screamed in frustration. During this devastating time, Aston brought me a consignment which was from dad. The contents of this consignment included a sealed envelope, cotton duck canvas roll, and a handwritten letter. In a frustrated mood, I took that letter into my hand and started reading it.

Letter

'Hi Joe,

How are you doing son? I miss you every day. Is the ocean still singing songs for you from its waves? I'm writing you this letter as a filler to your fragmented happiness. I was aware that you are struggling to portray your childhood memory. I know this because of Aston. Trust him always. In case I forgot to mention this earlier, here is the information which you need to know right now. Your mom owns a house in farming land at Flam village. We spent the spring of '95 at this farming estate, you, me, your mother, and her parents. It was a part of your mother's tradition, known as Spring pasture. You were the happiest then and almost explored the whole farm on bare foot. The memory of your joy that you are constantly trying to capture is from this place. I think you should revisit these farms soon. The beauty of this place would move even the most indifferent souls. That house was vacant, and the farm was not cultivated since the death of your mom's parents. So, there will be no problems for you from the people to spend some time in this place. I hope you will rediscover your fragmented happiness there and fill up this canvas with your emotion. I have already emailed that farm's address to Aston and am sending you an envelope which contains our photographs at that farming estate.

Good Luck,

Love,

Jeff.

While watching those photographs sent by dad, a photo displayed me (from my back) standing at a four feet tall flowering plant and desperately trying to catch its flowers. Staring at those fully bloomed flowers in the photograph, my mind started to dig deep to catch up one of my precious memories which was buried under the deep layers of my brain. . . This memory had presumably happened a few hours before to my existing childhood memory at the same location. .

.

That memory was.... 'As winds were blowing along with an alluring sweet fragrance across the surroundings, I was in a great crave to search for that fragrance. While exploring all around, I halted at a plant by finding beautiful flowers over it. Sensing the fragrance was intensified, it was obvious to me that the fragrance which I was trying to find was coming from these flowers. I tried to catch those flowers with great curiosity by standing on tiptoes. But I failed to take them into my hands, because those flowers were a bit high from me. Dejected, I turned back towards mom and asked her to assist. Halting to capture this moment in camera, she reached me with contentment in her face and lifted me up to the height of those flowers. Gently picking a flower into my little hands, I sniffed its aroma into my lungs'....

Concluding that this was the same fragrance which I had experienced while chasing the butterflies, my heart was filled with delight for eventually discovering the source of that fragrance. I decided to leave for mom's farming estate to get those flowers and to set up my past memory in full detail.

After throwing all the broken sketches and wooden easels into the bin, I headed out to Flam village that night. Along with me, I carried a sketch book, sketching tools, purees of paints, and a LED light pad.

ADULTHOOD - (DRIZZLE IN THE DESERT)

How does it feel when a person gets some warmth when stuck in freezing snow mountains? How will a person feel when it rains while he is in the middle of the hot desert? That's exactly what happened to me. When I started my journey to Flam, I did not expect that this outing would be the beginning for a whole new chapter in my life....

Reaching mom's farming estate in Flam, I parked my car in the shrubby bushes to keep my presence secret. Once I got down from the car, the scene over there looked completely different from my past. The wooden house which was at the edge of the farm seemed to be in a ramshackle shape. The farm was completely messed up with overgrown trees and grass, thick layer of leaves all over the ground, and broken farming tools lying scattered. I didn't expect such an unpleasant welcome from this place. I was totally disappointed at seeing the awful state of that location. But there was a tiny hope left in me that the plant would still be alive. So, I started to explore around the house and the farm in search of that plant.

But even after 30 minutes of searching, I failed to find it. Getting to the sense that it's difficult for any plant to survive in the harsh conditions of an abandoned farm, I gave up my search by concluding that the plant may have already been dead. As my desire to obtain that plant got shattered, I became upset.

'Why to get disappointed! If not here, I can definitely find that plant somewhere else.' I said this to myself.

Then, I decided to complete the remaining task of reconstructing my childhood memory before sunrise. When I opened my shoulder bag and was about to pick up sketching equipment, my wrist watch rang a beeping alert.

By listening to this alert, I slipped into a jitter. My heartbeat raised exponentially. My spine chilled. Unable to think what to do at that moment, I ran into that wooden house with my shoulder bag and locked myself inside. After a while, I heard vehicles' sounds and some faint voices. Terror-stricken, I peeped out of window to get a clear picture of what was going outside. In the farm next to my house, under the glow of flashlights, I saw a group of people unloading some camping gear and saplings from the pickup trucks. Terrified by seeing the presence of those people, I couldn't stay there. Though my mind warned me to leave that place immediately, I couldn't do it because those people could catch sight of me if I stepped out of the house. So, holding my fears within me, I remained in that house in absolute terror.

30 minutes later.... Sun began to rise and those group of people were in full swing to set up the camp. As the time passed by, few other people also joined and the kids started filling the camp. That place which looked so secluded until a few hours ago, now turned into a festival environment. While I was nervously thinking when this place would become empty, a spectacular scene caught my eyes in between that crowd fair....

Through the leaves of apple trees, sunlight was gleaming on the grassland in patches. Under that gleaming sunlight, I saw a beautiful lady who was teaching something about plants to kids. She looked more like an Indian with a slight Norwegian skin tone. Her height could have been around 5 foot 6 inches, and had a perfectly curved body covered in a skin fit white coloured t-shirt and sky blue Jeans. Her graceful heart shaped face was embellished with a slim nose and fetching lips. Increasing her prettiness to the next level, gently blowing wind had made her soft black hair to flutter around her cheek. . . 'Wow! Her beauty would definitely make Aphrodite feel envy,' I wondered. . .

Captivated by such a beauty, I kept peeping at her in a mesmerized state. But then, a stirring incident made her reach so close to my heart....

Beside that lady, there was a little boy who was trying hard to catch an apple which was hanging down from the tree. Noticing how the boy was struggling to catch the fruit, the lady went to the boy and gently lifted him up with a divine smile on her face. Reaching to the height of that fruit, that boy plucked it with great delight. While watching this, similar incident of mom lifting me to the height of those flowers ran through my mind. Forgetting all the anxiety in me for a moment, I was transfixed by a kind of satisfaction of witnessing the same kind of emotion which had happened between me and mom long ago. With this lovely scene that happened in front of me, my past incident with mom felt so fascinating. In a sudden jolt of inspiration, I picked up the tools and started to paint my past scene with mom.

Alongside the painting, I repeatedly kept peeping at that lady. Though many people were coming and going from that camp, my eyes were completely stuck to her. Perhaps more than her beauty, I might have been attracted to her as I saw my mother in her with that exquisite incident.

I spent the whole day rigorously churning out the painting. When the painting was almost finished, the smile on mom's face seemed a bit plastic. As my face had been covered behind the flower while sniffing its aroma, it didn't display any emotions.

Though I was not satisfied with the painting's outcome, I felt good about the painting because it stood as a sweet recollection showcasing the beautiful moment that had happened between me and mom.

Time was 8:20 pm, organizers of the camp packed all the camping equipment and left the place by then. As the place became empty, I was relieved. My house turned dark as the sun had already gone down. So, I lit up a lantern. Under the dim glow of the lantern, I engaged with the painting to conclude its final details.

5 minutes later, I heard someone calling, 'Excuse me....' As I sensed this voice very close to the house, I was horrified and turned off the lantern. Leaving the painting and other tools, I immediately hid under the table to keep myself invisible to the outsider if he looked into the house.

A while later, I heard the door knock. Holding my fear, I remained under the table and hoped that the outside person would leave the place if I didn't open the door. But that didn't happen, and after a while I once again heard a call of, 'Is anyone here...?'

I sensed this call from the other side of the window, which was next to the table where I was hiding. Following this call, I heard a loud thud from outside. I was startled by the sound and thought that the outsider was trying to infiltrate into the house by breaking the window. I was deeply worried. I then sensed a hammer at my feet. Picking up the hammer, I rushed towards that window and pushed it opened. I raised the hammer to throw it at the intruder, believing that the wounded intruder would flee from there. But the scene at the other side of the window seemed totally different from what I thought. There was a lady lying still on the ground. Seeing her white t-shirt and vaguely visible face in the dim glow of the crescent moon, I recognized who she was. She was the lady at whom I peeped all the while since morning. Looking at me, she screamed in horror. Perplexed and frightened by seeing her, I dropped the hammer to the floor and hid down at that window.

'Why did that lady come here? Did she notice me while I was peeping at her and come to quarrel with me? Oh no! What if she recognized me?' I was worried and decided to run away from there before she could catch me.

Right away, I stood up and ran towards my car to flee from that place. But when I reached my car, I realized I had left the car key in my shoulder bag. I then ran back into the house for the key.... But bizarrely, we both came together inside the pitch darkness of that house.

After some time, that lady asked me for cotton. Picking up the cotton roll from my painting kit which was on the table, I passed it to her. While dressing up her wounds, that lady introduced herself as Cherry. Then, she asked my name. With her sudden query, I got nervous and didn't understand what to reply? I couldn't say that I'm Edward Bell. I didn't get any name into my mind spontaneously. So, as my people call me Joe, I told her my name was 'Joe'. I said this because, world knew me only as Edward Bell, but not as Joe.

After completing to dress up her wounds, Cherry got excited by the paint bowls on the table and identified that those paints were made from the fragrance of Summersweet flowers. I was stunned and started to think how could she know about these flowers? Then, Cherry revealed that she was a botanist and also owned a nursery. By learning this, I became excited and tried to ask about that flowering plant which I failed to find in this farming estate. But being so anxious due to her presence, that query did not come out of my mouth.

When I was thinking how I could ask her about that plant, Cherry said that she left her handbag somewhere in the farms and was unable to find it. To find that bag, she requested me for a light. Grabbing the lantern, I turned on the fire hesitantly and kept it in dim mode. I kept the fire in dim mode because I feared that Cherry could see my facial details and identify who I was. In the soft glow of that lantern, I looked at Cherry's face. From such a close distance, that too in the soft orange tone of lantern fire, she looked more beautiful than morning. For the first time, I made eye contact with Cherry. My goodness! I never saw such expressive eyes neither in humans nor in paintings. There was a tiny mole beneath the corner of her left eyebrow, which stood as a dazzling emblem for her beauty. I was completely transfixed by her majestic eyes and kept glancing at them....

Even after exchanging looks with me, Cherry didn't recognize me. I felt so thankful for my altered look and the dim light around.

When Cherry turned towards the exit to go and find her missing bag, she spotted my painting. After studying the painting, she suddenly turned to me and asked, 'Did you paint this by watching me with that kid?' Having been caught by Cherry I wasn't able to find any other way to escape from her question and I agreed with her.

She then asked me whether painting was my profession?

'Yes...' I lied, to hide my actual profession.

Listening to my answer, Cherry smiled casually at me and headed out into the farms to look for her lost bag.

Even after a rigorous search, Cherry failed to locate her bag. Understanding her situation, I gave her money for travel expenses to reach her home.

Just before leaving the place, Cherry asked me whether I would return home along with her?

To evade this query and to prevent Cherry from questioning where I was living, I simply lied that the wooden house is my residence.

When Cherry prepared to leave, I turned so desperate to ask her about that flowering plant. But my anxiety forced me to stay silent as usual. Then, Cherry somehow understood that I was unable to open up and asked me if there was anything I wanted to say? As Cherry herself asked me this, I said that I needed to find a flowering plant and hesitantly requested her help. Accepting my request, Cherry invited me to her nursery garden on Saturday afternoon. As I could not step out during daylight, I said that I could only visit there at night. She agreed to this and left the place.

Believing I could get that flowering plant from Cherry's nursery garden, I felt so pleased. In this positive mood, I concentrated on constructing my childhood memory by sitting in the place where it happened. The glow of the crescent moon provided me just enough light to read that location. Placing the papers on the LED light pad, I sketched a few thumbnails by reading the surroundings.

These thumbnails contained every detail of that location and a vague sketch of my childhood figure chasing butterflies in that location. Picking up all those newly made sketches and other remaining stuff of mine, I left for the island.

Keeping those thumbnails as references, I started to paint my childhood memory excitingly. I kept working on my childhood figure and left the background portion empty without applying any paint, because I still needed to get that flowering plant.

It had been 2 days since I had seen Cherry. I sent my heart along with her. No no, it's not at all normal for a tough guy like me to simply send my heart with a woman. Instead, I must say that she had stolen it. I found myself so strange because my agonized life never gave me a chance to develop feelings on a woman other than my mom. Even twinkling stars above my head appeared lifeless when I recalled her mesmerizing eyes. . . 'Hmm! Did I connect to Cherry by seeing my mother in her with that kid's incident? Or did I connect to her because of her majestic eyes and beauty? Knowing her profession, did I get attracted to her believing that she could help me in finding whatever plant I need? Maybe, it could be the combination of all these which made me fall for her.' I thought to myself. . .

Counting every hour, I eagerly waited to meet Cherry at her nursery on the following night....

It was Saturday evening, and it was time to leave for Cherry's nursery. If she was a normal woman, I would have simply sent Aston to bring that plant. But she was not like any other woman, she was something special. My heart craved so intensely to see her. I felt her eyes could show me the purest emotions. I strongly believed that the joyful emotions in her eyes could help me to portray the true joy in the eyes of my ongoing childhood painting. So, though being hesitant and anxious, I left to meet Cherry.

Since I saw Cherry at the nursery's entrance, I couldn't keep my eyes away from her magical eyes. Feelings in her eyes looked as deep as the ocean. I was completely drowned in that ocean in a state of trance. But interrupting this pleasant mood, Cherry turned on the lights once she took me into the greenhouse. Till then, the soft dim light which was present around us, suddenly turned too bright, and I was terrified.

Cherry asked me what plant I needed? I showed her the photograph sent by dad and asked for the flowering plant present in it. Then, I came to know about the difficulty in finding that plant through Cherry. I was utterly disappointed. But Cherry assured to help me in every possible way to get that plant. She then asked me whether I want to see any other plants...? In reply, I asked for some berry plants and coloured leaf plants as I needed to prepare colours for my painting. After searching for a while, I managed to find only 3 of them. When I asked for the remaining plants, Cherry said that those plants were out of stock for now and they would arrive soon.

After finishing packing those plants, Cherry expressed a doubt that she had previously met me somewhere other than in Flam! Frightened that she may identify me, I denied and left the nursery with the plants.

In addition to Cherry, I also took Aston's help to get that rare plant. Aston kept contacting plant smugglers and black market dealers but failed to find that plant.

On the other hand, I kept working on my painting. Every now and then, in the nights, I continued to visit Flam farm to get some inspiration for my painting.

4 days later.... Cherry dropped an email mentioning about a new stock of plants arriving at the nursery, and that I must come, and pick

up the ordered plants. As I was eagerly waiting for our next meeting, I agreed to visit nursery the following night.

When I went to nursery the following night, I saw a group of customers purchasing the new stock. I waited for more than 30 minutes in my car for the exit of those people. But the customers continued to grow and their constant movement around my car made me scared. So, I left from there.

Next night when I visited the nursery, Cherry was angry at me. She revealed that she went to Flam farm in the morning to pick up her car and to handover those plants to me. Cherry furiously said that she failed to find me there and came to know that I'm not a resident of that wooden house. She doubted that I was hiding something from her and furiously queried who I was...? As Cherry caught me red handed, I couldn't evade her query. Being liable for causing trouble to her, and feeling that she was close to my heart, I felt bad for hiding the truth from her. So, I revealed who I was. Cherry initially didn't believe what I was saying. But after a while when she recognized me, she was greatly surprised. Then, I invited her as a guest to my island to make a deal regarding the plants. . . 'There was also another selfish motive for inviting her to the island'. . . Accepting my request, Cherry agreed to visit my island.

Upon reaching the island, I showed my paintings to Cherry and explained my signature style of inducing smell and sounds in the painting. Cherry was excited to learn this. When we sat with a cup of coffee, I mentioned to Cherry that, being a celebrity, it was very difficult to make a visit to the nursery. So, I requested her to help me by bringing the wanted plants to the island for preparing colours. I had a selfish motive behind asking this. That motive was to spend time with Cherry at the island itself whenever she brought the plants. So I don't need to visit the nursery for her. While I eagerly waiting for her response, Cherry agreed to bring the plants to the island. With her acceptance, I was delighted.

Cherry often visited the island with the plants I asked, and we both spent some lighthearted moments together. After Cherry's exit, I used to sketch joyful emotions which I observed in her eyes, and utilized these sketches as references to extract the joyfulness in the eyes of my childhood painting...

Our bond blossomed along with the time. Cherry treated me like a dear friend by ignoring my stardom. This made me even closer to her. I tried to express my feelings for Cherry. But my inexpressive nature, and fear of how she would react, didn't let me.

While I was struggling to express my love, one night, I visited Flam farms. After spending some time at the place where my childhood memory happened, I decided to return to the island. When I was getting into my car, I suddenly got an idea that could help me in expressing my love for Cherry. That idea was to find her lost handbag in the farms and to place a proposal letter in it. Believing that this was the perfect way to express my feelings for her, I started searching for that bag at the place where that camp happened. After an hour of hard searching, I finally saw it covered under the grass.

Upon reaching the island, I took a piece of paper and wrote my innermost feelings for Cherry and placed it inside that hand bag.

Though I failed in expressing my feelings for Cherry directly in person, this letter conveyed to her what I wanted to say, and Cherry accepted my proposal.

One evening, while spending intimate time together, I intended to make love. But Cherry didn't show interest because of being in period. Understanding her problem, I gave up my wish.

As time flew past, I was deeply engaged in painting my childhood memory. I started to feel that the emotion in my childhood face was not turning out as desired. Cherry suggested that if we could do outdoor painting sessions by observing the joyful faces of kids, that could make the painting work. Frightened to step out, I strongly disagreed with Cherry and continued to paint behind the closed doors of my island.

With passing days, Cherry became frustrated with me for keeping myself locked in the island. She asked me to accompany her in search of the Diamond of Kinabalu orchid plant. But reluctant to step out, I insisted Cherry to go and find it alone. She rejected my proposal and was determined to find the plant only with me. With Cherry's refusal, I could simply send Aston to search for that plant. But at this point of time, he was in Malaysia looking for that plant. As there was no other option, I reluctantly agreed to step out with Cherry in the nights.

ADULTHOOD - (BLUNDER)

We searched that plant for two nights, but failed to find it. On the third night, after finishing the search, Cherry revealed that it was her birthday. She wished to celebrate her birthday with me in Geiranger village and took me there.

After reaching Geiranger, Cherry stopped the car in a remote place and we got down. I was tense due to the new surroundings and kept an eye on that locale. On the other hand, Cherry put up the camp tent and started preparing dinner. While having dinner, Cherry tempted me to make love. Initially, I didn't show any interest as I was totally dominated by my fears for being in an alien place. But then, because of Cherry's aggressive approach, I couldn't restrain myself and joined in. Just when we were about to have intercourse, my watch sounded an alert, suggesting that there was someone around us. Listening to this alert, all the concealed fears within the walls of my heart exploded in a fraction of a second. At this time, the only thought that ran in me was, 'What If those people spot us and recognize me alongside Cherry! That will not only reveal my identity, but also smash Cherry's privacy into pieces. By tomorrow morning, this would become a massive headline in every newspaper in the world'. I slipped into extreme panic. My body started to shiver. My palms became numb. My scared mind thought not to take a chance when Cherry was alongside. So I decided to flee from there with Cherry as soon as possible. I didn't even check whether I pulled up my clothes properly! There was no time to think about the clothes on our bodies. There was no time to explain what was going on to Cherry. I pulled Cherry forcefully towards the car in great fear and she kept on resisting me. As I kept pulling Cherry, she slapped me. With the slap, I left her hand. My watch kept on ringing, suggesting that those people were coming closer and closer. I was terrorized and ran away from there in my car, leaving Cherry behind.

BACK TO PRESENT

Recalling this devastating incident, I suddenly woke up from the bed. Thinking of my painful past and the blunder I committed, I was completely depressed. Alas! My committed sin doesn't go anywhere. It will keep haunting me all the time throughout my life. This unbearable guilt, and Cherry's absence brought me all the way to Agra to pacify her rage over me and to bring her back into my life. But now, everything ended with my failure in the concert. Though I tried best to prove my change, as always my fear of people put me down in the concert.

Because of my failure at the concert, I was in anguish. My agony was not because of failing in front of people but remaining a failure in front of my woman. Now, there was no way left to gain Cherry's trust again. My heart started to feel this was it, and I couldn't take it anymore. I slipped into extreme despair and started ripping the room and everything in it into pieces. While I was wrecking my room, a gun dropped down from the broken wooden drawer. Seeing that gun on the floor, I turned calm. As all my blunders and enormous torment kept squeezing my heart, I couldn't bear the pain anymore and sensing that Cherry could no longer forgive me, I decided to break free from this unbearable pain.....

EXCITING NEWS DURING THIS DEVASTATION

In this deeply distressing time, I learned an exciting news. This news was about Diamond of Kinabalu orchid plants which were found in a nursery garden named 'Green Treasures', located at Thenzawl town, in a state called Mizoram. Feeling that time had given me one final chance to convince Cherry by obtaining that flowering plant myself, I gave up the attempt of suicide. After knowing the information of that plant, no matter how difficult it was, I decided to get it, because after my failure in the concert this was the only way to prove my change to Cherry.

As I decided to leave for Thenzawl, I went to dad's room to announce my departure. Once I entered the room, I saw dad on the couch. He was taking whiskey in a dejected mood. I walked to him and sat next to him on that couch. Dad poured some whiskey in a glass and offered it to me.

'No thanks.' I rejected his offering. 'Dad, I have one thing to say,' I said in a low pitch tone, looking downwards at the floor.

'Yeah, please....' Dad granted me permission to talk and sipped whiskey in the same dejected state.

'I'm leaving for Thenzawl tomorrow morning.'

'What...!' Dad reacted instantly in disbelief and left the whiskey glass to ground in a state of shock.

'Yes dad, what you heard was correct. I'm going to Thenzawl.'

'Do you understand what you are saying...?' Dad said in the same shock.

'Yes. I'm saying this in full consciousness. I can't have another chance,' I replied.

'No Joe. Don't talk foolishly.'

'Enough dad. I failed in my life. I failed in the concert. But I don't want to stay as a failure in front of my woman. Now the only way left for making Cherry trust me was to prove to her that I can face this world by going to Thenzawl and getting the plant myself. If I still succumb to my fears and don't go there, there's no meaning for me in being alive,' I stated.

By listening to these words, dad remained silent without opposing my decision. He didn't try to stop me from going to Thenzawl nor gave me any encouragement for reaching there. Maybe, as my well-wisher, he could have been very happy with my decision. But the father in him may have worried about how I would deal with it! This could be the reason for his silence. Because of my achievements, dad often used to say that he was so proud of being my father. . . 'Dad, I will make you proud once again by heading out and acquiring that plant'. . . Saying this to myself, I held dad's hand and gently squeezed it (Indicating that I was committed to the decision I took, and I will live up to it). Gesturing this, I walked off from there.

JOURNEY

To keep my identity hidden during the journey, I altered myself to look like I had done in Norway. I then packed my stuff. Thenzawl was 2250 kilometres away from Agra. It takes around 3 days for me to reach there. So Aston booked the hotels (which were on the way) for my night stays. Hotel bookings were done on the name of Joe to keep my actual name and identity hidden. Only the managers of those hotels were informed who I really was. I know that staying in hotels was not going to be easy for me. But I decided to face the challenges no matter how difficult they were.

Dad offered me a smartphone and said that it would help me in guiding me towards my destination in this alien country. Though I was afraid to use the phone, I took it, feeling what dad said was correct. I set my destination in that phone's map and began my long journey to Thenzawl in the Jeep-Compass just before dawn.

On the vacant roads of the early morning, I stepped hard over the accelerator and crossed the city when the sun was about to rise. As spring had already set in, trees sprouted with new leaves, same like the change that sprouted in me. The greenish paddy farms which were on either side of the motorway looked very charming. In this greenery, under the glow of the rising sun, I saw a herdsman with a bright red turban driving the herd of sheep. This visual seemed like a beautiful scene painted on a canvas. I felt good to see such attractive visuals on the way. But this pleasurable feeling didn't last long as the Indian motorways started to pack up with vehicles from 7 AM.

After four hours of drive, I entered a city called Lucknow. Driving in this city felt like hell because the roads were flooded with vehicles and people. Seeing these crowded roads, I felt busy London streets were way better than these crammed Lucknow roads. Accustomed to drive in the nights of vacant Norwegian roads, I felt anxious to handle this heavy traffic. After an hour of difficult driving, I finally managed to cross the city.

Two hours later.... Because of driving since morning, I felt a bit tired and hungry. Needing a break, I stopped the car at the roadside. I ate pre-packed lunch which contained a meat bun and steak pie. After having lunch, I sweetened my mouth with Duffy's chocolate. My energy spiked up with this lunch break and I continued my journey.

I drove until 10:00 PM. Since I was driving continuously, I was fatigued and couldn't continue anymore. My body desperately needed rest. I still have to drive another 15 kilometres to reach Muzaffarpur, where my hotel was booked. Following the directions in my phone, I drove towards that hotel.

Once I reached the hotel, manager received me. He completed the check-in formalities and took me to my room. This was the first time for me to stay in a hotel and I felt so anxious. Despite my anxiety, I slept well that night. With this good sleep, my fatigue was completely wiped out and I was revived to start my new day. This experience of staying in hotel gave me the confidence that I can deal with any odds in my journey. I took the steering wheel at 7:30 Am and continued my journey....

After a 9 hours of drive, I reached a city called Siliguri. This city greeted me with a huge sign board, 'Welcome to the gateway to Northeast'. Upon seeing this board, I felt delighted as I entered the northeastern part of the country. Though I had to travel another 1050km in this northeastern part, I felt I was nearing my desired flowering plant with every passing mile. 20 kilometres after crossing the city, I entered rolling hills which were entirely covered with terraced tea gardens. While driving through those tea gardens, I saw a couple in front of me travelling on a bike. While the guy was riding the bike, his woman was hugging him. I felt so jealous as there was no Cherry alongside me and I was travelling alone without her. Feeling envious to see them, I increased the speed of my car and overtook them. After 5 minutes, while I was in the same envious mood, I saw another couple sitting on concrete railing at the edge of the road in the backdrop of those lovely rolling hills. As the man rested his head on the shoulder of his woman and playing with her hair, she was pampering him. This reminded me of the past times with Cherry, as I had done the same while lying on her shoulder. Ah! How beautiful could my life be now alongside Cherry if I did not commit that sin. How happy could be Cherry, if I was like every other guy without any disabilities. But I was not like any other guy. I was the guy who brought all the agonies to my woman. No one couldn't even imagine how much pain I caused to Cherry. Could anyone forgive me after knowing what I did to her? Recalling those dreadful times, my mind took me to the past....

BACK TO PAST

ADULTHOOD - (GOOD TIMES AND GREAT DISASTERS)

After Cherry left me because of the mess I made on her birthday night, I felt so disgusted with myself. I deeply regretted what I had done. Unable to face Cherry directly, I sent her gifts and letters for the following week expressing my regret. But I did not get any response from her.

As this process kept going, on the other hand, I continued to paint my childhood memory by locking myself in the island, and Aston took responsibility for finding that flowering plant in absence of Cherry. At the halfway point of my painting, I started to feel that my childhood face on the canvas showing up a plastic laugh instead of great joy. I was frustrated and vigorously kept modifying the laugh of my childhood face, but the result did not change. Failing to depict the genuine joy on my childhood face, I turned furious. Unable to control myself, I showed that fury on my painting and tore it to pieces.

Few minutes later, while I was in dejection for failing in my painting, Cherry visited me. There was a bunch of letters in her hand along a transparent tote bag which contained gifts I sent to her.

'Damn! Why are you still disturbing me? Don't ever try to patch up my heart by sending these fucking gifts,' said Cherry as she threw all those letters and gifts at me.

When my failure in the painting put me in total distress, this wrath from Cherry hurt me even more. Suppressing that pain within me, I said, 'Cherry, I'm so sorry for what I did'.

But she showed no mercy on me and ranted, 'Enough. I don't need your apologies anymore. I no longer want to see your face and pursue any type of relationship with you. If you send me any gifts again, my response will not be lenient anymore, mind it.'

Making this warning, Cherry walked away from me. While stepping out of the room, she spotted my broken painting at the corner of the room. Picking up that broken painting to her hands, she turned back at me.

'Are you mad! How can you do this after working so hard for days! Oh! This is not new to you, right. You can easily break anything. On my birthday night, you broke my heart. Now you have broken your own painting. Why did you do this???' Cherry queried, fumingly.

'No matter how hard I tried, I failed in portraying genuine joy. That's why I destroyed it,' I replied in a lamented mood.

'Well! Without stepping out and pursuing happiness, how can you successfully portray joy? Come out of the island first.' Cherry ranted at me.

'How can I do that? Can you ever forget what happened when I came out on your birthday night.'

'What's your problem Joe? I can't understand what you are fearing for...? Tell me about this, do you have any mental issues???' Cherry questioned me bluntly.

Mental issues... As Cherry asked me about this, I painfully started narrating how the freaking world had pushed me into this plight. From obtaining stardom to losing my private life, from how the world made me dreaded and how I went to dark, from quitting my career & hiding in Oakril, I revealed everything to Cherry. Her face turned sorrowful after knowing all this.

'People don't know that I am living a secret life here. Once be in my position and think Cherry. What if we were seen and recognized! How bad could the consequences be? I did not understand what to do at that moment. So I fled from there in fear, but I didn't mean to hurt you,' I said in regret.

'Oh no! Joe, why didn't you tell me about your past all these days? Why didn't you tell me that you left your career? I thought you took a break from music and were relaxing here.'

'If you know my painful past and the fact that I left my career and hiding here, I feared that you would see me as a failure who didn't cope with the difficulties and ran away from the world. I feared that you would leave me by knowing my disabilities. That's why I didn't tell you about this. I'm sorry for hiding this from you Cherry.' I said in remorse.

'I thought you were the culprit for my birthday night's mess. But now, after knowing about you, I grasped the fact. You are not a culprit Joe, you are a victim. I can now understand what made you behave that way on that night. I am really sorry, I was harsh on you.' Cherry said with a pitiful tone.

I felt so grateful to Cherry as she turned soft towards me even after the mess I created on her birthday night.

As days flew past, the damaged relationship between us got mended. We became closer to each other than ever before. I shared all my feelings with Cherry. There are no secrets between us now. Cherry knew my weaknesses, and I knew hers.

One day... As a symbol of our love, Cherry brought Carnation plants and a Red Rose plant from her nursery and started planting them in the island's flower garden. Getting many flowering plants except Diamond of Kinabalu orchid made me dejected. While Cherry was busy planting the plants, standing next to her without giving any help, I went on thinking if I could ever get the Diamond of Kinabalu orchid???

'What are you thinking Joe? Come and help me.' Cherry urged.

I joined Cherry. Planting along with her, I asked in despondency, 'Cherry... Can we ever get Diamond of Kinabalu orchid?'

'Oh! Come on Joe, we will. Please don't give up hope,' Cherry said, comforting me.

'Although I get those flowers, can I successfully portray the true joy of my childhood memory?' I said in despair, recalling my failure with the painting.

'Since you are living far from the happiness and missed the beauty of your childhood, you are failing to capture the right amount of joy behind the laughs and happiness of your childhood memory. If you want to find success in painting, come out from the island and pursue the happiness around,' said Cherry.

I replied nothing as I couldn't do what Cherry said, and carried on to plant along with her.

As I expressed despair for not finding Diamond of Kinabalu orchid, Cherry desperately inquired about that plant. After two days of intense effort, she came up with the information of where we could possibly find it - at a renowned orchid collector in Myrdal, and in a nursery at Vossevangen. I was greatly excited upon knowing this. I strongly desired to get it and start my painting again. So, I called Aston and he came to my room.

'Hey Aston... You know what, Cherry finally got the information of that plant. You right away go and bring it,' I said excitingly.

As soon as I said this, Aston looked at Cherry. They both communicated something with their eyes. Then, Aston looked at me and said, 'No Joe. I can't do anything in this matter. I can't go.'

'What...' I said, baffled, as Aston opposed my proposal for the first time ever.

'Cherry has already told me that she wants to go to those places along with you. I cannot upset her. Sorry, I cannot go.'

'Now you have no other option, Joe. Pack your stuff, we are leaving tonight,' Cherry said.

'No Cherry... No... I am not coming.'

'Ok. If this is your decision, you need to know mine as well. I am not going to those places without you whatsoever. And I'm sure that Aston will not go there either. Aston, what's your take on this?' Cherry asked Aston.

'Yeah Cherry... Your decision is my decision.' Aston said bluntly.

I was shocked by listening this. What a traitor was Aston! Ignoring our camaraderie, he joined hands with Cherry and refused to go. With Aston's refusal, I agreed to head out with Cherry as there was no other way left for me to get that plant.

As my island was about 380 km away from those two places, Cherry planned our stay in Flam farm's wooden house. She selected Flam because this village was just a little distance away from Myrdal and Vossevangen, so that we can easily go to those places from there.

We started our journey to Flam at 7:00 pm and reached there around 1 a.m. Cherry and I worked hard for over an hour in cleaning the wooden house's bedroom and turned it into a good stay. As the room got cleaned, I went to bed. When I was just about to slip into sleep, Cherry stopped me with a harsh pat on my shoulder and said, 'Did we come here to sleep? Wake up, you lazy guy...'

What will anyone do at midnight without going to bed? I didn't understand why Cherry rattled on me for sleeping!

'Please Cherry... Let me have some sleep.' I said to Cherry in drowsiness and pulled up the blanket to my face.

But Cherry didn't allow me to sleep and dragged the blanket from me. I have no idea why she was suddenly going this crazy!!! While we both were fighting over my sleep, I heard the sound of a car stopping in front of the wooden house. I was terrified by this sound and peeped through the window to find out why and who halted the car. Surprisingly, I saw Aston getting down from that car. I didn't understand why Aston was here? I didn't understand what was going on? While I was in this confusion, Cherry in a super excited state, went out of the house and met Aston. They both started unloading paragliding equipment from the car. I was stunned by seeing that paragliding equipment.

'Why did Aston bring this paragliding gear here?' This doubt was raised in me.

Immediately, I perceived it was because of Cherry. I then understood the reason why Cherry kept me from sleeping. Though I know Cherry was a champion in the paragliding sport, I never even thought that she would plan something so unimaginable. That night in Cherry's company, my long-held desire came true....

Hundreds of feet above the ground, under the soft glow of greenish aurora borealis and twinkling stars, I flew in the skies while Cherry operated the paraglider behind me. In the silence of that midnight, with tall mountains on either side, this experience of flying in the sky felt like a dream. When I stared down, I saw valleys consisting of woods hundreds of meters beneath my feet. It looked like my legs were hanging down in the empty sky and an excitement burst out in me. I didn't scream out in that excitement, but calmly lived the moment with great pleasure. In this pleasure, I reminded birds flying in the skies and said to myself that I was flying like a bird now. It was a precious moment when the unfulfilled desire of my life came true. I was so thrilled and contented to fly like a bird....

After a good 10 minutes, we slowly headed towards the ground. Once we touched down, a kind of gratitude pumped out towards Cherry and I kissed her for what she had done. I didn't even thank Cherry, but this kiss would have clearly stated to her what my feelings were. Cherry made my day by accomplishing my desire to fly like a bird.

The following morning... Some faint voices and laughs nearby awakened me from sleep. Startled by these sounds, I peeped out from the window to know what's happening at my place. Outside of the wooden house, right in the middle of the farm, I saw half a dozen village kids playing with Cherry. I was frightened and irritated with the presence of those kids. When I was in this frayed mood, Cherry stepped into the house.

'Hey Joe, how long has it been since you woke up? See who's in the farm, come and join us.' Said Cherry.

'Are you mad! Why did you allow those kids to the farm?' I fumed on Cherry.

'Calm down baby. Spending time with those children could help you to depict the genuine joy in your painting. That's why I gathered them for you. Come, let's have some great time with them.'

'Keep your mouth shut Cherry. I am not coming anywhere.'

'Joe, please listen.....' Interrupting Cherry, I said in rage, 'Stop it Cherry. There's nothing to hear from you. All the kids should be out of here in a minute. Just get out of my sight and do what I said.'

As I refused to join those kids and rebuked Cherry for bringing them, she got hurt. But strangely, Cherry did not show any irritation towards me like in the past and dispersed those kids from there. Because of this, I felt that Cherry had started understanding me after knowing the past life of mine.

A while later... Cherry and I were engaged in preparing bread omelette for breakfast. 'Joe, what shall we do after having breakfast?' Cherry asked while roasting omelette.

'Get the plant,' I replied.

'What...! Time is only 8:20 am. Nursery will not be open until 10:30 am. Why go there so early?'

I said nothing and took the roasted omelette and bread to my plate. I sat next to Cherry on the kitchen platform and started having breakfast.

'Let's do one thing Joe. Let's spend these 2 hours hiking in the valley. Weather outside looks stunning.'

'No. Don't talk rubbish. I am not coming anywhere.' I refused Cherry's request irritatingly because I was scared to step out during daytime.

'Joe please... Let's hike...' She pleaded.

'No... If you are that interested, you go and hike,' I said at Cherry, annoyed.

Cherry was disappointed as I turned down her wish. She had her breakfast without speaking to me. She then went to the bedroom and started working on her laptop. I took a nap in the hall.

I woke up at 10:00 am. The nursery in Vossevangen was about to open in 30 minutes. As I was scared of stepping out during the day, I decided to ask Cherry to go and get the plant. I went to the bedroom. Cherry was still looking irritated, working on her laptop. As I rebuffed her wish of hiking a while ago, I didn't understand how to ask her to go and get the plant. I felt abashed.

With my presence in the room, Cherry looked at me angrily and said, 'What...?'

'Hmm... Cherry...'   I faltered, feeling abashed.

'Tell me, what do you want?'

'Will... will you go to Vossevangen and get the plant?'   I asked hesitantly.

'Idiot. Don't you have any shame to ask this. Listen, if I am going to Vossevangen or Myrdal, that is only with you,'   said Cherry angrily and continued to work on her laptop.

With this harsh reply, I understood that she would not go there without me. I had no other option except to accompany Cherry if I wanted that plant. Although my fears were holding me back, I said, 'Ok Cherry, I will come. You go and get ready'.

We got ready. Cherry took the steering wheel and we left for Vossevangen. We traveled through the beautiful fjords, cascades, tunnels and Naeroydalselvi river. Under the daylight, the landscapes on the way seemed stunning. It felt good to see such scenic places. . . 'Perhaps for showing me such breathtaking nature around, Cherry might have brought me out,' seeing the lovely landscapes, I thought to myself. . . Savouring the beautiful places on the way, we reached that nursery in Vossevangen. Cherry asked me to accompany her to the nursery. But I refused her request and stayed in the car. Cherry went alone inside. After 10 minutes, she returned with empty hands.

'Cherry... Where's the plant?' I asked.

'They sold it last evening,' Cherry replied sadly.

'Damn!' I said inwardly in disappointment. 'Cherry, did you ask whom they sold it to? We can buy back the plant from that person offering a fancy price.'

'I asked. But they said they don't know the customer details.'

I was completely upset by listening to this. As we failed to get that plant in the nursery, now the only hope left for me was that orchid collector in Myrdal.

We left for Myrdal. My mind ran through a series of thoughts both good and bad in obtaining that plant at Myrdal. With these thoughts, we reached there. As usual, I stayed in the car and Cherry went inside to meet that orchid collector....

15 minutes later, Cherry returned. She said that she found the plant, but it's a sapling. Being aware that it takes twenty years for that sapling to mature and bloom, I was devastated as my last hope in getting its flowers were ruined.

Returning to the wooden house, I sat down in a state of despair. 'Show some smile on your face Joe. It's hard for me to see you in this depressed mood,' said Cherry in a tender tone while consoling me.

But ignoring her, I remained glum.

'Let's forget what has happened and enjoy this outing. . . Joe, have you realized this? You have not even sung one single song in front of me. I want to listen a song from you now,' said Cherry, intending to bring me out from this dejection.

'Cherry please, leave me alone for some time.' I said in despair.

Then, Cherry unwrapped her clothes. 'If this can cheer you up, I am ready to join you in bed,' she said, offering herself to me.

I was shocked at what Cherry did.

'No Cherry... I cannot do this. It's a matter of your self-respect and this will happen only when you desire it from the bottom of your heart, but not in a sympathized way as a relief of my despondency,' I said, turning down her offer.

Due to Cherry's act, I understood how strongly she was intending to bring me out from this dejected mood. So, to divert my saddened mind, I went for Cherry's other proposal of singing a song rather than having sex. Instead of singing any of my old songs, I decided to make a new song for Cherry. I felt she deserved this because of her love and support for me. Reminiscing my times with Cherry, I started to croon alongside playing piano in her mobile.

Song:

I remember those times, when there was only pain in my life
I remember those times, when there was no hope
But then, everything began to change
Who ignited light in my darkness
Who soothed me when I was in pain
That's only you,
Only you, yeah

When I was stuck in loneliness
You came in, and showed me new modes of life in your affinity
When I was fearing this world
You took the roll of my guardian angel and guided me through
Did I ask you for all this
But you did, yeah

Long ago, I had my heart set on to fly like a bird one day
But that never happened until you arrived
Did I ever even dream that this will come true
Could anyone even believe that what I'm going through was true

How could I thank you for this
What could I do for you for this
Except to love you more and more
And to adore you furthermore.

'How strange the time could be! When I failed to get that plant, it gave me a heartwarming song instead.' With this song, in a moment of epiphany, I understood what Cherry had brought into my life and how beautifully my times have changed with her arrival. I did not want to leave this song and wished to make it big. So I rushed back to the island with Cherry.

Holding on to the lyrics, I sang the song in a soft tone and composed music by combining the genres of Soft-pop and my Edwardzee style. I was so contented with the overall outcome of the song. The lyrics and composition in this song reminded me of the glory days of my career. After a decade of unsatisfying tunes, the excellence of this song ignited a spark in me and I decided to film it. So, I got back to my old popular look by clean shaving my overgrown beard and cutting my long messy hair to neat 4 inches. Cherry loved my transformed look and asked me to continue in this groomed shape. I was fond of Cherry's beauty, and in the same way Cherry had every right to be fond of my handsomeness. So respecting her wish, I decided to carry on with this look. I don't know how long I would keep this look, but what I knew was, Cherry will be very happy as long as I continue in this look.

Setting up all the available equipment, we started to shoot the song in the open landscapes of my island. Cherry and Aston were the only people who were involved in filming, and I was the only character to appear in the song. In collaboration with both of them, I finished the song's shoot and its post-production work in a week.

Final outcome of the song exceeded my expectations. I was so pleased to get such a grand result. My life took an awesome turn with the arrival of Cherry and I even made a song that lived up to my potential after so many years. I couldn't be happier. To celebrate this occasion, and to thank Cherry for making this fantastic song possible, I planned something special....

Under the pinkish aurora sky, in the island's flower garden, Cherry and I came together for that special ceremony. In the moment of accomplishment and delight, I opened the expensive champagne bottle which dad sent me 2 years prior. In the span of these 2 years, I did not find a happier time than this to open the bottle, and I celebrated this moment by spraying champagne on Cherry and all around cheerfully.

After this enthusiastic celebration, we settled on the chairs in that garden by facing each other and started having that champagne. While Cherry was sipping champagne, I took out a gift pack from my coat's pocket and offered it to her.

'What's this???' Taking that gift into her hands, Cherry asked me in excitement.

'Please open it,' I said in a tender tone.

Once Cherry unwrapped the decorative cover, she saw my song's CD and her face turned puzzled.

'If you did not ask me to sing a song on that day, this song wouldn't be possible today. Cherry, I'm dedicating this song to you. I strongly feel that you deserve this for not only making the song happen, but also for bringing beauty into my life.' I said in a thankful tone.

I expected Cherry to become crazy in delight as I dedicated this song to her. But contrary to my expectation, Cherry turned quite emotional by broking down into tears.

'Cherry... What happened?' Seeing her shed tears, I asked in a perplexed mood by holding her hand.

She replied nothing, but stood up from chair by placing the champagne flute and CD upon the table.

While I was looking at her, she came to me and settled in my lap. Grabbing me into her hug, she kissed me in same shed tears. This clearly stated to me how happy she was for dedicating the song to her. My delight doubled for getting such an overwhelming response from Cherry. Her smooch made me so aroused and I kept kissing her in great passion. While kissing, Cherry unwrapped my coat and removed my shirt. With this advancement from Cherry, desire of making love erupted out in me. I lifted Cherry into my arms and walked towards the open bedroom from that flower garden. I laid down Cherry on the bed in that open bedroom. Gazing into her seductive eyes, I removed her frock. This exposed Cherry's gorgeous body. Her breasts were hiding their glamour beneath the bra, and her privates were covered with pantie. My looks stuck to her thighs as they looked so erotic. As the pink tone of the aurora sky reflecting all over her semi naked body, I stared at her in a sense of astonishment. Because of this aurora spectacle over Cherry's skin, her staggering beauty multiplied countless times more than normal. Seeing my woman in such a staggeringly sexy state, I became mad. I bent down at Cherry and took her navel into my hands. Rubbing my cheek against her soft navel, I kissed her bellybutton. Moving upwards, I licked her skin around the bra. Sensing my tongue upon her breasts, Cherry moaned by cuddling me firmly. As I continued to lick around her breasts, she turned so amorous and pulled down my trouser. Equivalent to this, I took off her bra and pulled down her pantie. With this, Cherry turned completely naked. Inevitably my eyes pointed towards her naked breasts. Because of the ocean breeze, her hair kept fluttering all over the breasts and her nipples hid in shyness beneath the strips of her hair. Using my fingertips, I gently moved those hair strips away from her breasts, making her nipples fully visible. Excitement arose in me by seeing her nipples and I kissed them by pampering her mushy breasts. I then reached down to her crotch. Her privates seemed enticing with nicely trimmed pubic hair. Softly pampering over her privates with my fingers, I kissed her there. Feeling this sensation, Cherry groaned by grasping my hair firmly. I continued the naughty play with my tongue over there and this act of mine floated her boat. She got up in great passion and kissed me so intensely. This kiss went too deep and we both even swapped our saliva. In the same intensity, Cherry kissed me all over. I was fully aroused by her foreplay and could not hold myself anymore. I removed my underwear and entered her. When I did this, Cherry gasped in pleasure. I then began to stroke her. Cherry kept moaning and clutched my butt with her palms. In the cool ocean breeze, her palms over my butt felt so warm. Cuddling Cherry, I continued to stroke. Observing this immense pleasure between us, mother nature turned jealous and started to pour out its envy. . . 'Ocean waves started to splash the island in great force. Wind started to gust and the branches of the oak tree above began to jiggle violently. Because of this, leaves of the oak tree dropped over us continuously. But the precious moment between us projected this envious aspect of nature in an entirely different way. As the outrageous ocean throwing its waves in peak strength towards the island, this defined the lust which was currently overflowing in us. As the wind making oak tree's branches and leaves to jiggle, this sound sounded like a background score for our lovemaking. As oak tree leaves falling over us due to that wind, it felt like nature was greeting us for our ongoing precious moment. All these combined, envious nature's rage actually made that moment more enjoyable'. . . Relishing this nature's deed during our love making, I continued to stimulate Cherry with my strokes. After a good 10 minutes, I reached climax and so did Cherry. This ejaculation gave me an ecstatic feeling. In this heavenly feeling, I fell asleep by cuddling Cherry.

Next morning.... Cherry got ready for her work and we both joined for breakfast. The morning's special was a full English breakfast and we started having it.

'Had a great night, right.' Cherry said merrily and took a spoon full of fried mushrooms to her mouth.

'Yeah...' I replied.

'I did not expect you to dedicate the song to me. Thanks for honouring me with such a great gift.'

I smiled at Cherry while having bacon.

'So when are you going to release the song?' Cherry asked.

'Why are you asking me this! Don't you know that I decided long ago not to release any of my songs?'

'What! Do you want to constrain the song same as you behind the walls of this island?' Cherry asked in shock.

'Look Cherry... If I release the song, I will get a lot of attention from people which will ruin my life again. I have done the song only upon my own interest, and there's nothing to do with its release.'

'No Joe, I don't want this song to remain just between us. If you really want to dedicate this song to me, release it as per my wish. That's how I would want the song to be dedicated and......' Interrupting Cherry in the middle, I bluntly said in irk, 'Enough. Don't try to convince me. I have already decided, and that was final.'

Cherry turned upset with my reply and left from there without finishing her breakfast.

For the following two days Cherry didn't show up at the island. But her dismay did not last long and she visited me on the third day. I knew Cherry couldn't live without seeing me longer than this, and I felt happy for her arrival. On that day and for the next few days, Cherry continued to urge me to release the song, but I kept dismissing her request. Due to this obstinate stand from me, Cherry may have perceived that I would not fulfill her wish whatsoever and stopped asking me to release the song.

Though I didn't deliver Cherry's wish, it didn't affect our bond. Cherry was as sweet as she always was, thanks to her understanding nature. Despite our minor quarrels, our affinity grew stronger with time. Our bodies were two, but the soul was one... One fine day, we made a decision to live together and Cherry announced our relationship to her people. But comprehending my concerns, and to avoid an instant buzz among her people, Cherry didn't reveal who I was to them. Her people only knew that Cherry was going to live with Joe. But what they didn't know was that Joe was Joseph Edward Bell. Cherry thought of revealing about me to her people later once everything got settled.

Cherry relocated to the island and we both excitedly started our live-in relationship. I wanted to keep Cherry always happy in this new life. But that didn't happen because of my disabilities....

One day, Cherry desired to spend some good time with me outdoors. Alongside this, she planned to plant some flower saplings as a memory of our love across the places where we had spent sweet times in the past. Cherry intended that these saplings would represent our love. But as I switched to my popular look, I refused to step out from the island even at nights due to my easily recognizable identity. Because of this, Cherry was utterly disappointed and headed out alone to plant those saplings.

As days passed by, I kept myself constrained to the island and Cherry stayed alongside me by giving up all her desires. Many times, I noticed her suffering due to my stance. But Cherry never showed any disappointment or rage at me. If Cherry was a normal woman like others, she could simply break up with me. But Cherry was not like any other woman. She was a beautiful soul who understood me deeply. I felt so grateful to Cherry for staying behind me even though I was causing so much pain to her.

In Cherry's affinity, days passed so quickly and winter arrived. With the climate change, Cherry's grandma came down with bad flu and Cherry went home to take care of her. It felt so burdensome for me to be away from my woman. As I do not use mobile, there were no words between us to fill this gap. Remembering Cherry very often, I spent ten days without her. These ten days of gap between us seemed like a lifetime and I pined for her so desperately. Unable to bear her absence anymore, I decided to pay Cherry a visit.

That midnight, when the world was in deep sleep, I reached Cherry's house. As I could not ring the doorbell which would wake up Cherry's grandma, I thought of an alternative. Then I got an idea. The idea was to wake up Cherry by calling her from nursery's phone. Keeping an eye on the surroundings, I nervously jumped the nursery fence. Straightaway I went to billing counter shed and slid open its window. I stretched my hand inside to catch up the cordless phone from the nearby table. Grabbing it, I dialed Cherry's number. Her phone kept on ringing, and after many rings, she finally lifted my call and said 'Hellooo' in drowsy state.

By hearing Cherry's voice after 10 long days, a kind of emotion struck me and I remained dumb without speaking anything.

'Hellooo... Whoo's this?' Cherry's tone sounded in the same drowsy state once again.

'Cherry, it's me,' I tried to respond. But that inner voice didn't come out from my mouth in that emotional state.

When I was in this dumbness, Cherry's voice excitedly sounded, 'Oh my god! Joe...'

Following this exclaim, a light was turned on in one of the rooms in Cherry's house. Opening that room's window, Cherry looked towards the nursery. . . 'For a moment, I didn't understand two things. Though I didn't even speak a single word, how Cherry identified me in the phone call? And how did she know that I was calling her from the nursery? It didn't take long for me to get the answers for these questions. The phone that I was calling from must have indicated to her that I was in the nursery. Except me, who would call her at midnight from the nursery's phone. Surely, Cherry may have identified it's me because of this'. . .

Catching the sight of me in the nursery, Cherry opened the main door and came out of the house. Seeing her, I was emotionally charged. My eyes filled in tears. Unable to hold myself, I dropped the phone to the ground and rushed towards Cherry. Reaching her, I hugged her tightly. . . 'Well! How powerful was love! It even made such a hard person like me so emotive by seeing my loved one after many days'. . . Completely forgetting that I was outdoors, I continued hugging Cherry with tears oozing from my eyes.

It took a while for me to calm down from this outburst. Once I calmed down, Cherry quietly took me to her bedroom without disturbing grandma's sleep. We both sat on the bed. I was so anxious thinking how Cherry's grandma would react if she saw me.

Recognizing my anxiousness, Cherry asked, 'What are you worrying about?'

'What if granny sees me?'

'Don't worry. I will take care of it,' said Cherry.

'How's her health now?'

'Much better than before. There has been no fever for 3 days. But still, she is weak. It may take some time to recover completely,' Cherry replied.   After a while, Cherry said in a melancholic mood, 'It has been so difficult to be apart during this time, right'.

'Yeah...' I nodded by gazing into Cherry's eyes which were filled with the pain of our separation.

'I never thought you would come. Thanks Joe, thanks for being here,' Cherry said in an emotional tone.

I left a tiny smile in response. We carried on with heart-to-heart talk of how these ten days went on. We shared some romantic time by kissing and cuddling. Past ten days of accumulated agony eased up by spending this good time with Cherry.

Time turned to 5:00 am. I decided to leave before granny woke up. Before sending me off, Cherry went upstairs to bring her jacket as snow was pouring outside. When I was putting on my shoes, granny entered the room suddenly, (Cherry showed me photos of her family members on mobile a long time ago, this is how I knew it was granny). I was terrified by granny's sudden arrival and I immediately pulled up my hood to hide my face from her.

'Hey! Who the hell are you...' Granny's threatening voice struck me.

I didn't know what to say. And as I was completely terrified by then, I ran away from granny for Cherry's aid (thinking she was the right one to deal with this situation). But granny caught me from back and shoved me to the floor. Picking up a dust cleaning stick from the door side, she started to hit me by yelling, 'Cherry.... Cherry.... Where are you? Come fast. There's a robber in the house'.

Though granny looked frail, her hammering felt rock solid. While she kept hitting me ruthlessly all over, I yelled at her in pain and terror, 'Please... please hold on. I am, I am no robber'.

Because of our yells, Cherry entered the room in great haste. She was shocked by seeing what was happening!

'No granny... Please stop, he's not a thief.' Cherry shouted at granny and halted her from hammering me.

'Oh god! Joe, are you ok???' Cherry said worriedly by taking me into her arms.

Deeply shocked by the incident, I remained petrified without even replying to Cherry.

'Oh granny, what have you done...!' Cherry's voice raised at granny.

Looking at both of us in a puzzled state, granny asked Cherry, 'Do you know him?'

'Yes... He's Joe. He came to see us.'

'Joe... Oh no! Which means is he the guy with whom you are living! I'm, I'm so sorry. I thought he's a thief as he covered his face with hood and ran away after seeing me.' Granny said to Cherry in remorse.

Cherry slowly raised me up from the floor and aided me to sit on the bed. Cherry gave me a bottle of water and I gulped it. Because of granny's assail, I felt pain in my shoulder, wrist and leg. But thankfully, there were no serious injuries. Fearing to make any eye contact with granny, I sat with my head down.

'I am extremely sorry Joe.' Granny's guilty voice reached my ears.

I didn't respond to granny. I didn't even dare to look at her.

'Granny.... Tell me this, why did you come here from your room?' Cherry questioned granny in an irksome tone.

'When I woke up, I didn't see you beside me on the bed. I thought you went to the bathroom. But later I realized you were not in the bathroom. In search for you, I came to this room and saw Joe inside.'

Though I was covering my face with hood, as there was no beard and long hair now, granny expressed a doubt by staring at me, 'Joe... I can feel you so familiar. Surely, I have seen you somewhere else previously'.

I was extremely worried as granny expressed this doubt. Not knowing what to do, I remained the same way with my head down.

'Joe... Let's tell her the truth. We should anyway reveal this at some point of time, right.' Cherry who was next to me whispered at my ear.

'Yes granny, you are right. You have seen him many times in his songs. I think because of the hood covering his face, you couldn't recognize him fully. He's Joseph Edward Bell.'

'Joseph Edward Bell! You mean, star of the music world?' Granny said in shock.

'Yeah...' Cherry conformed.

Granny came to me and pulled off my hood. Gazing at my face with her eyes wide open, she said in disbelief, 'Oh my god! Cherry, you are right. He is Edward Bell.' Then granny looked at Cherry and said, 'I can't believe this...! Are you in relation with him! But why did you keep this as a secret all these days?'

'That's a big story, and I will explain about it later,' Cherry replied to her.

As granny knew who I was now, I thought it was better to get out of there before she started asking me any further questions. So I got up from bed and said to Cherry, 'It's already late. I should leave now'.

'Yeah, ok.' Cherry replied. Cherry then said to granny, 'You go to bed. I will be back after sending Joe off'.

'What! Where will he go now? Snow is pouring outside. It's better to stay back for now and start at noon,' said Granny.

Though my heart wished to stay with Cherry, presence of granny, and the embarrassing moment which took place between both of us made me quite abashed. So, ignoring granny's suggestion to stay, I set off for my island.

For the following three days, I was confined to the island though my heart wished to meet Cherry. My reason for not visiting Cherry was granny. I was embarrassed to face her because of that nasty incident.

On the fourth day, Aston said that Cherry called him and requested me to pay her a visit. Though I was desperately willing to visit Cherry, feeling embarrassed and my nervousness in facing granny didn't allow me to go there.

For the next two days, I got the same request from Cherry again and again. With these entreaties from Cherry, and with my craving to see her, I left for Cherry's house sheepishly while pondering how I could deal with granny? But once I reached there, granny received me very genially. This cordial reception from her put me at ease. All three of us had a light-hearted chat and it seemed like granny had already forgotten about what had happened between us during our last encounter. Once granny went to bed, Cherry and I had wine together. We had a lot of chit-chat. We made love. After having this wonderful time at night, I returned to the island in the early morning.

Ever since that day, I regularly visited Cherry in the nights. During these times, grandma interacted with me so affably and we both slowly developed a good bond. Granny's friendly nature made me quite comfortable in dealing with her. In a week, granny became a trustworthy friend of mine who could keep all my secrets. Granny treated me like a person at home, and I completely let my guard down around her. I was so happy to have a person like granny in my life. I started to spend my time at Cherry's home during the daytime as well. When Cherry went to the lab for work, I used to stay with granny. During these times with granny, I learned how to cook Cherry's favourite dishes, watched my albums alongside granny, helped her in making some artifacts with the waste materials around, and never forgot to give medications to her. My time with granny passed very sweetly. Cherry brought many beautiful aspects into my life, and I felt granny was one of them.

One day, leaving me and granny in the house, Cherry went to a nearby school to conduct an awareness camp on plants for kids. When I was in Cherry's room, I saw a photo album inside the table drawer. Taking the album, I started looking at the photos in it. The photos captured the jolly times of Cherry's family from the past. While I was busy looking at the photos, granny entered the room. Sitting beside me, she narrated the sweet moments of her family during the time of taking those photos. Seeing such a happy family, I felt curious to know why they all got split up suddenly after Cherry's mother's death?

'Granny... can I ask you something?' I said in a bit of hesitation.

'Sure...' She permitted.

'Why did your family split suddenly after Cherry mom's death?'

'After my daughter's death, Cherry's father could not live here with her memories. The same time, his father passed away in Agra. Unable to live here and to look after his family's marble business after his father's death, he moved to Agra along with Cherry's brother. This house which saw our togetherness for eighteen years, eventually left with two of us.'

'Why did Cherry not go to Agra with her father?'

'She loves me so much. So, she did not want to leave me here alone. Her father forced her to come with him. But she didn't agree. I lost my daughter, but Cherry stayed along with me as a daughter. However, Cherry did not keep away her father either. She often goes to Agra to visit him. That's her commitment towards loved ones.' Granny said in tears with pride.

I felt proud of Cherry after listening to this from granny.

'Joe, I want to tell you something... Cherry was the only one who brought me out of misery when I was struck hard with my daughter's death. She was an angel of my life. And I am sure she will be the same to you as well. Take care of her all your life, and please never make her suffer. This is the only thing I'm expecting from you.' Granny said in a soft affectionate tone.

I couldn't respond to granny. I couldn't respond because, Cherry was constantly suffering in every aspect because of me. Meanwhile, the doorbell rang. Granny went and opened the door. It was Cherry who came back after completing her camp. On that day Cherry seemed so special after knowing what she had done for granny, and my respect towards her increased substantially.

Few days later.... Granny completely recovered and stayed in good spirits. She herself told us to leave for the island and that she could very well take care of herself. As a send-off party, granny planned a grand dinner for Cherry and me. Without even taking our help, granny herself made delicacies such as Farikal, Steamed salmon, Lapskaus and Lefse.

All three of us joined for dinner. While I was having Steamed Salmon, granny offered me a small gift box and asked me to open it. I paused to eat and opened that box excitingly. Inside that box, I saw a tiny guitar made from match sticks.

'Oh! Looks cool. Thanks granny.'

'This should remind you of all the beautiful days that happened between us,' said granny.

'Granny, how can you stay here alone? I think it's better if you come to the island with us.' I asked granny.

'What do you mean? Are you thinking I cannot live here alone? Joe, you are underestimating my bravery,' she said, a little angry.

'No no. I didn't mean that. What I am saying is.....' Interrupting me, Cherry said, 'Granny... How could he underestimate your bravery after your onslaught over him on that day'. Saying this, Cherry laughed.

Following Cherry, granny also bursted out laughing.

'Granny, do you know this... Something similar happened when Joe and I met for the first time in Flam.'

'Really...!' Granny said and paused eating.

'Yeah. I almost hit him with a stick. He was lucky enough to escape on that night. But luck didn't favour him with you.' Cherry said in smirk and had a spoon full of Lapskaus.

'Granny... You simply hammered me that day. I will not forget that incident in my life.' I said to granny and smiled.

Listening to this, Cherry laughed again.

'Good to see you guys in this happy mode. Stay like this all the life.' Granny said by seeing smile on both of our faces.

'Definitely, we will.' Cherry said confidently at granny.

'When granny asked me never make Cherry suffer, I was left with no answer. But Cherry, without another thought, immediately assured granny that we will live happily. Well! Can I live up to Cherry's expectations? Or will I break her heart as always...?' I thought within me, feeling bad about myself.

After completing the dinner, Cherry and I prepared to leave. Picking up all the stuff, we reached the main entrance along with granny.

'Whenever Cherry visits here, you should come with her.' Granny said and hugged me.

'Yeah, sure...' I replied.

Following me, granny hugged Cherry. After this warm farewell, we both got into the car. Cherry took the steering and I settled beside her. Starting the car, Cherry drove forward....

Nearly after 2 hours of drive, we were just 11 km away from the island. There were tall mountains across the road and winter filled them with snow. Passing by those beautiful mountains which were glittering under the greenish aurora sky, Cherry stopped the car abruptly at the roadside.

'What happened? Why have you stopped the car here?'

'Wow! See how beautiful this place is. Come, let's get down and enjoy the place.'

'No... Don't talk foolishly. Start the car,' I said, annoyed.

'If you don't like to step down, stay inside.' Cherry replied in irk and got down from the car.

Standing in that location by herself, Cherry started to take selfies. On the other hand, I locked myself in the car. After taking selfies, instead of returning back to the car, Cherry walked forward. Reaching a small bridge (which was approximately 35 meters away from the car) she leaned forward on that bridge's railing and began to enjoy the beautiful nature around. Time kept ticking, but Cherry didn't show any interest in returning. After a couple of minutes, I decided it was late and got down to bring Cherry back to the car.

When we both were returning to the car, a red Audi R8 came and halted behind our car. A man got out of that car and took out a camera. Frightened by seeing him and a camera in his hand, I pulled my hood further down and hid my face using my palm. Immediately I rushed towards my car by pulling Cherry with me. When we reached my car, that man who was busy setting something in his camera, glimpsed at us. Noticing this, I experienced great terror. Without wasting any time, I got into the driving seat in panic and Cherry took the front passenger seat. Starting the car in great haste, I drove forward.

'Fuck! Did that man recognized me?' I worriedly thought while driving forward swiftly. Five minutes later, when I was still in this concern, I saw the same red Audi R8 approaching us at great speed from behind. With that car nearing us, my mind strongly suggested that the man had recognized me and was following us. Suddenly my anxiety multiplied. To evade that tailing car, I stepped further hard on the accelerator and reached hazardous speed.

'Oh no! Joe... what are you doing? Slow down the car,' Cherry shouted at me in a worried state.

'Shh! Shut up and sit quietly. That bastard was following us,' I said anxiously while driving forward like lightning.

'No Joe... Please slow down. If that person had an intention to follow us, he should have tail as soon as he saw us at that place. But he didn't do that. Believe me, he was not following us,' said Cherry in an extremely tensed tone.

Totally ignoring Cherry's outcry, I continued to drive in dangerous speeds as that car kept coming closer to us.... After nearing my private road (which leads towards the coast building), I turned the car into that road at great speed. Then I realized that the tailing car had headed straight on the main road and was not a threat anymore. But due to high speed in that turning, and skiddy road in winter, I lost total control on the car and rammed it into a tree with a loud bang sound in addition to Cherry's scream. In a split second, air bags from all sides blew out. And then, everything turned dead silent. After a second of silence, my ear caught a faint moaning sound from Cherry. Though I was in pain due to my own injuries, I feared most of what happened to Cherry! In utmost worry, I looked at her. Leaning against the curtain airbag, Cherry showed up in severe pain.

'Cherry... are you ok?' Collecting all my strength, I asked in extreme bother by gently patting her cheek.

But except of moan and cry, there was no response from her. I could see a few bruises and cuts over my body, except for that no severe damage happened to me. But Cherry's condition seemed completely different to me. As the impact was on her side, she was wounded badly. Seeing Cherry in such pain, I was heartbroken. Although I was desperate to help her, what could I do? Could I take her to hospital myself? My damn fucking fears don't let me to do that. As I couldn't take Cherry to hospital, I decided to seek Aston's help. I picked up Cherry's mobile and unlocked it with her fingerprint. I then called Aston....

Before any help arrived from Aston, I managed to get out of my broken car. While I was trying to bring Cherry out, Aston along with two of my private security officials rushed to the site. All four of us carefully pulled Cherry out from the car. Aston took her to hospital and I went for first aid in island.

Next day... Through Aston I came to know that Cherry had a fractured leg, broken ribs and neck strain. Aston further mentioned that Cherry went through surgery to her fractured leg. Knowing Cherry's condition, I was quite rueful as I put her in absolute hell. I condemned myself for what I had done to Cherry. I found no other way to atone for my mistake except to be with Cherry and take care of her in these painful times. Although I desperately wanted to be with Cherry, my fear of people didn't allow me to go to hospital and I was completely fucked up because of this.

4 days later... Cherry got discharged. That night, in desperate yearning to see Cherry, I went to her house. While just about to ring the doorbell, I stopped. I stopped for fear of how granny would react after seeing me as I was responsible for the mishap. Gathering my courage, I rang the doorbell tentatively. Few seconds later, granny opened the door.

'Hey Joe. Please come in,' Granny warmly invited me inside with a smile.

Strangely she seemed in a calm state instead of being furious with me. I was baffled and stepped in while wondering, 'Why granny was so amiable towards me even after I put Cherry in such a suffering?'

Once I was in, granny gazed at me and spoke in a bit of concern, 'Thank God! Nothing serious happened to you in the mishap. But I heard that you have suffered some minor injuries! Are you fine now?'

'Yeah... I'm fine. What about Cherry?' I asked, by still thinking why granny was so tolerant towards me!

'It may take a month or two for her to walk,' replied granny in a pity tone.

'Where is she?'

'Resting in her room? Go and see.'

I walked tentatively towards Cherry's room thinking how she will receive me! Once I entered the room, I saw Cherry on the bed. With a neck support band, gauze covering the stitches of operated leg, and bruises on cheek, she looked pathetic. Seeing Cherry in such a terrible state, I was shattered. I dolefully reached the bed and sat on it beside Cherry. With my presence, Cherry turned her eyes away from me in repugnance. Noticing her disgust over me, no words came out of my mouth. In deep regret, I then gently touched her hand as a sign of apology. But immediately, she took her hand away from me and said in disgust, 'Did you come here to see whether I'm still alive?'

I was heartbroken by listening to this from Cherry. Controlling my tears, I said in remorse, 'Cherry... I'm... I'm sorry'.

'How many times have you said this to me in the past! Did anything change? Enough Joe, I don't need your apologies anymore. You even made me fear for life when I'm with you.'

I was shattered by what Cherry said. Tears started oozing from my eyes.

Taking her hand into my palm, I pleaded with Cherry remorsefully in tears, 'I'm extremely sorry Cherry... Please tell me what can I do to wash this sin? Shall I get you the best doctors? Round the clock care? Tell me, what can I do?'

Taking a while of gap, Cherry said, 'Will you really do what I ask???'

'Yes....' I replied.

'Then release the song. And I want your change, I want to have a great life with you. Please Joe, I want you to overcome all your fears and live like every other guy by stepping out from your confinement. Our lives should not be constrained behind the bars of the island or this house anymore. These are the only two things I'm expecting from you,' said Cherry in tears by holding my hand.

I turned silent by listening to these demands from Cherry.

'Joe... Please promise me that you will live up to these wishes.' Cherry pleaded by staring into my eyes.

I didn't respond to her. Because I knew I could not fulfill these wishes. Meanwhile granny entered the room with a dinner bowl. Placing that bowl on the bed side table, granny handed over to me some medications and said, 'Don't forget to give these pills after Cherry has dinner.'

'Sure...' I replied.

'What about you? Did you have dinner?' Granny asked me.

'Yeah... I had it before starting.'

'Ok. I will be in my room, call me if anything is needed.' Granny said and walked off the room by shutting the door.

'Why is granny so amiable towards me! I thought she would fume over me for succumbing to my fears and causing the accident.' I asked Cherry in a puzzled state!

'She would be, if she knew the truth...'

'What do you mean...!' I asked Cherry in bafflement.

'I said I was driving the car at the time of the accident,' she replied by looking downwards.

I was shocked with Cherry's answer. I felt so bad for hiding the truth from granny.

'Cherry, I can't take it. I have to tell the truth to granny.' I said to Cherry in a lamented mood and got up from the bed to go and tell the truth to granny.

Immediately Cherry caught my hand and said, 'No Joe. If you say the truth to granny, I will never see your face again'.

'But why, why do you want to hide this from granny?'

'Because I don't want to make you bad in front of her. I don't want anyone to blame you for this. Please Joe, please do not reveal the truth to granny,' pleaded Cherry.

'Damn! Do I still deserve your mercy? Cherry, tell me this... How can you be so compassionate to me even though I'm causing many sufferings to you?'

'Because I love you. Because I still believe that you will change. Please Joe, promise me that you will never surrender to your fears again. And I want that song to be released. Your love towards me shouldn't remain just among us, it should reach all corners of this world through this song.' Said Cherry emotionally in a soft tone with tearful eyes.

My heart melted by listening to what Cherry said. I fell into a catch-22 situation as I could not smash Cherry's hopes on me, and could not put myself into trouble by fulfilling her desires.

'I... I will surely consider these,' I replied to Cherry hesitantly. Though I said this, I had no idea of what I was going to do in this matter....

Days passed, but I didn't make any effort in making Cherry's requests possible. Spending time between my solitude at the island and visiting Cherry in the nights, I completely neglected Cherry's wishes.

One night, while Cherry was still bed ridden, I visited her house. Standing on the doorstep, I knocked on the door. But granny didn't open it. I waited for a while, and then, I rang the doorbell.

'Who's that..?' Cherry shouted at the top of her voice from inside while the door remained shut.

With Cherry's bawl from inside, I thought granny went out somewhere and for that reason she was not showing up at the door. Since I had a spare key, I opened the door and went in. When I stepped into Cherry's room, I saw her in an extremely worried mood.

'Cherry... What happened? Why are you so anxious?'

'Granny went to the pharmacy over an hour ago, but hasn't returned yet,' Cherry replied in panic.

'Ok. Please relax and call her.'

'I called her. But she left her mobile here. She should have reached home by this time. But she didn't. Joe... my mind is suggesting something bad.'

'Oh! Come on Cherry... Maybe granny didn't find a taxi in time to return back.'

'Both pharmacy stores are just a mile away from here. Even if she didn't get a taxi, it hardly takes 30-35 minutes to go and return home by walk. Oh dear! But she hasn't returned yet. Definitely, something bad has happened to granny.' Cherry said in an anxious tone by looking downwards. Then, immediately she raised her face at me and said, 'Joe, do one thing... You go search for her at local pharmacy stores. One of the stores is in church street, and the other one is opposite the bus station'.

'What...!' I replied in shock to Cherry's demand.

'There is no other way left for us now. Even staff at the nursery have headed back to their homes. So please Joe, please go and search for granny in those places,' Cherry urged me in great worry.

'No Joe... No, you can't do this. Please do not agree...' My mind strongly warned me.

Though my nervous mind was pulling me down, I decided to head out by seeing Cherry's concern. In addition to this, I felt not to remain as an absolute zero in front of Cherry by putting her in a helpless state during this tense time by succumbing to my fears. So, ignoring my mind's warning, I headed out to find granny in the utmost panic state.

Firstly, I drove to the pharmacy store at the bus station. Reaching there, I investigated that store for Granny from inside my car. But she didn't show up in that store. Failing to find granny there, I drove forward slowly by searching for her in the neighbouring vicinities. Even after exploring that entire area, I didn't find granny anywhere. Concluding that she might have gone to church street pharmacy, I turned my car towards it.

While I was just about to reach the church street's pharmacy, I spotted granny resting on a bench in a weakened state and five people tending to her. As I found granny, I pressed my foot against the brake and the car stopped. With the presence of those people alongside her, I didn't understand what to do! . . . 'Come on Joe... What are you still waiting for? Go, go and bring granny to the car.' My heart instructed me. 'Fuck! But how can you do that with people around her???' My mind countered and held me back. . .

While I was in a quandary about what to do, a middle-aged man who was beside granny rushed towards my car. I was terrified to see him coming to me. Reaching to the passenger side window, he knocked it. If it were normal times, I would have simply ignored him and rushed forward. But it was a situation where I couldn't leave granny on the road. So I covered my face with a hood and lowered the window glass ever so slightly instead of fully opening it. I did this to prevent that person from fully looking into the car, so that he couldn't get a clear picture of mine.

'There is an elderly woman in weak state. We got no cab to take her home. Can you help us drop her off at her house?' That man asked while trying to peep inside the car.

I thought that he would bring granny into the car if I agreed to his request, so that I could remain inside the car hiding from those people. Holding my nerve, I said to that man, 'Yes... Bring her in'.

'Thank you...' Said that man and ran back to granny.

With the assistance of another man, he gently lifted granny from the bench and slowly led her towards my car by holding her hand. Opening the back door of my car, they kept granny's handbag in, and then, they gently led granny to sit in the back seat. Once they put granny in, they shut the door. When those two people were about to reach the other side of my car to get in, I stepped hard on the accelerator and moved forward at rocket speed. While proceeding ahead in that great speed, I looked into the rear-view mirror and noticed those people sprinting behind my car shouting at me to stop. After a while of chasing, unable to catch up my swiftly moving car, they gave up. As I got away from them along with granny, I felt relieved.

When we were on the way to home, granny suddenly indicated pain in her chest and collapsed on the seat. Noticing this, I immediately stopped the car and turned back at granny. She was unconscious. She was flooded with sweat all over her face. I was thrown into panic at seeing granny in such a terrible state. I stretched towards granny from the front seat and patted her shoulder by squawking, 'Granny... What happened? Open your eyes and look at me...'

But there was no response from granny. I thought it was a heart attack. I was horrified. I didn't understand what to do!!! I thought of calling Cherry to seek help. But since there was no mobile with me or granny, I got no help. Now it was up to me to decide what to do. As I was running out of time, I made up my mind to take granny to the hospital by myself. The only hospital I knew in Volda was Volda trust hospital, which was about 1.5 miles away. I regularly passed this hospital while coming from the island, that's how I knew its existence. I started to drive to that hospital while deeply worrying about how I could deal with the people there.

On halfway to the hospital, a massive carnival blocked my car and didn't give me any scope to go ahead or reverse. I got trapped along with granny. I was so scared of the carnival crowd. I was so scared of granny's condition as well. I cannot be late in taking granny to the hospital. While I was worriedly thinking how I could make it to the hospital, I saw a bunch of police vehicles a few distance away. Since the road was completely jammed with crowd and I had no chance of driving the car forward, I decided to approach the police, thinking they would help me in taking granny to the hospital by clearing the blocked way. I found no other option.

I covered my face with hood and got down the car. Hoping that no one should see my face, I put my head downwards and started walking towards the police. My walk felt unsteady as my hands and legs were trembling with fear. People's burbling around me and loud beats of carnival music sent shivers down my spine. As I was walking with my head down, I bumped into a woman. This caused my hood to slip down and exposed my face. I was horrified and shielded my face with my palm to hide myself. I even pulled up my hood using the other hand. Despite these attempts, the damage was done as the people around recognized me. I suddenly became the centre of attraction to the people and completely overshadowed the ongoing carnival. In no time, I was mobbed by them. Shrieking in excitement, people fell over me by clicking selfies and photos. Their shrieks and wild behaviour petrified me. I was drowning in sweat even in the bone chilling cold. I felt my heart was beating abnormally. My vision turned blurry. I became extremely dizzy and I felt I was about to faint.

'Granny got stuck in the car. Please, someone help,' I tried to tell the people before I faint. But I passed out prior to saying this.

A few minutes later....

When I opened eyes, my vision appeared blurred. I blinked my eyes 3-4 times to get a clear sight. As I did this, my blurred vision cleared up and I saw a doctor and nurses around me. I didn't understand where I was and what was going on!!! It felt like absolute chaos. I turned my eyes away from them and saw some medical equipment all around the room. That was when I realized I was in hospital. I was frightened. I started thinking why I was in the hospital. In no time, my brain recalled what had happened to me and I realized that I must have been brought here after fainted. I was terrified what happened to granny, who was trapped in the car. In urgency to learn about her situation, I stepped down from bed while still feeling dizzy. But the nurses didn't let me go out and put me back to the bed. I said to them that granny got stuck in my car, unconscious. They passed on this information to the nearby emergency services to bring granny to the hospital. Then, doctor performed some tests on me. Seeing the test results, doctor said that all my vitals were fine and I fainted due to 'Vasovagal syncope' induced by stressful event.

10 minutes later... Granny was brought to the hospital by the paramedics. She was rushed to the emergency room and I waited outside it in extreme nervousness. After some time, the doctor came out. Looking at me in bemoaned state he said, 'I am sorry Edward. She was dead on arrival. It was a cardiac arrest. It could have been better if she was brought to the hospital early.'

I was devastated by listening this. I had no words to speak. If I had reached the police, they might have assisted me in bringing granny to hospital in time and granny could have survived. But that didn't happen as I succumbed to my fears and fainted. How bad was granny's fate. Although I fainted, she could have survived if someone saw her stuck in the car and brought her to the hospital. But the tinted windows of my car might not have allowed people to see granny trapped inside. Hence, she got no help. Police came and recorded my statement upon granny's death and completed the formalities.

I was shattered by the incident. My inner voice accused me for granny's demise. Unable to show my face to Cherry, I went to the island. I locked myself in my room. My words went mute and my tears stood as emblems of my torment. My heart kept on blaming me as a murderer. I spent two days with grief and remorse in my room.

The next day, I learned through Aston that granny's funeral was taking place. Feeling that it was my moral responsibility to pay final tributes to my beloved granny, I went to the funeral.

At the cemetery, I saw Cherry in a wheelchair, being comforted by her people. Still recovering from her own injuries and unable to cope with the loss of her grandmother, she was visibly devastated. Observing this from a distance, I was heartbroken. Unable to hold out against this disturbing visual, and frightened to face Cherry's people, I headed back to the island without even paying tribute to granny.

Upsetting visual of Cherry's breakdown at granny's funeral kept on haunting me, and I was absolutely shattered. . . 'Oh! Poor Cherry. What good had happened to her because of me? I broke all her dreams. I almost cost her life with that accident. And now, I took away her remaining happiness along with granny. Even after committing such a sin, I didn't pay tribute to granny and haven't sought any apology to Cherry. Can I forgive myself for all these blunders? Do I still deserve to be a human? No I don't. Because I'm a rogue. I am the rogue who smashed my woman's life and caused her immense agony,' I reprimanded myself for my blunders. . .

Unable to get rid of my sin towards granny and unable to bear the unthinkable suffering I left to Cherry, I was utterly rueful. My silence continued for days and my tears didn't leave me. My heart carried on blaming me for granny's death and I was infuriated with myself. As this sin kept crushing me, I desperately craved to meet Cherry for a chance to apologize. So, I drove to Cherry's home.

Reaching there, I saw a bunch of cars parked outside her house. Seeing the cars, I learnt that there were people inside her house. So, I didn't dare to meet Cherry and returned to the island.

I often used to go to Cherry's house to meet her. But due to the continued presence of her people in the house, I didn't get a chance to meet her.

On the eleventh day.... I, as usual, reached Cherry's house. Till the previous day, nothing seemed strange at Cherry's house except the presence of her people inside and their cars parked outside. But now, the scene has completely changed. Instead of parked cars, there seemed a truck in front of Cherry's house. Some of her stuff was already packed and kept in that truck, and remaining equipment was being transferred into the truck by the workmen.

'Where's Cherry going...? Oh no! Is she leaving the town! I have to meet Cherry now at any cost to know what's going on.' I thought to myself in deep concern, by observing the whole scene from my car.

After completing to load the stuff, all the workmen got into that truck and left the place. With the departure of that truck, Cherry's parking turned empty. There was no other car present there except of Cherry's. Concluding that this was the right time to meet her, I got down from my car. Meanwhile, Cherry came out of her house and locked the main door. She was accompanied by another woman who was of her age. After locking the door, they both walked towards Cherry's car. When they were about to get into the car, I called Cherry from behind and ran towards her, though the presence of that woman put me in extreme bother. As soon as I reached Cherry, she raised her hand in rage to slap me. But after bringing her palm so close to my cheek, she abruptly put down her hand without slapping and said in tears of fury and frustration, 'Grrr! You don't even deserve this... Before I do anything insane, just leave from here.'

With such a harsh reaction from Cherry, I was traumatized. With tearful eyes, I said in a saddened tone, 'Cherry I'm sorry. I.....' Interrupting me, Cherry shouted in wrath, 'Shut your mouth up... There's nothing left to hear from you. Only because of your disabilities, granny is no more today. Hey listen... The greatest mistake which I made in my life was to love you. And I cannot afford to lose anything more because of you. Goodbye...'

Saying this, Cherry turned from me and said to that woman, 'Anna... Go start the car'.

That's when I came to know that the woman was Anna. Cherry often used to say that she was a great admirer of me. But there was not even a slight elation in Anna's face with my presence. Instead, her face was filled with intense disgust towards me. I never saw such an atrocious reaction from a fan. And I felt I truly deserved this for what I had done to her dearest friend.

Following Cherry's insistence, Anna stepped into the car. When Cherry was about to get into the car, I stopped her and said in remorse, 'Cherry wait... Please give me one final chance. I will never make you suffer again. From now on, I will definitely do whatever you wish.'

'If you really want to do what I wish, then please get lost from my sight right away.' Cherry shouted in repugnance and opened the car door to get in.

'Cherry please don't say that,' I said in a shattered mood by holding her hand to stop her from getting into the car.

'Leave my hand.' Cherry said in rage while trying to extract her hand from me.

But I didn't leave her hand.

'I said leave my hand.' Cherry's enraged tone struck me again, this time with much more intensity in her voice.

'No Cherry, I will not. Tell me, where are you going???'

Shoving me back (thus freeing her hand from me), Cherry exploded by saying, 'Far away where I could never see your face again. Far away where granny's absence and her memories don't ruin me. Hey you listen, you can never change. Continue to constrain yourself behind the walls of the island and die in your darkness.'

Stating this, Cherry got into the car and locked the door. I immediately rushed to the car. Tapping the window and pulling the locked door, I pleaded, 'Cherry please don't do this to me. Open the door.... Open the door....'

But ignoring me, Anna drove the car forward. For some distance, I ran along with the car by banging the window and pleading Cherry not to leave. But then, unable to catch up with the speed of the car, I stumbled and fell on the road. In front of my eyes, the car raced ahead into the steep turning and disappeared. Though Cherry went away from me, I didn't give up. To stop her, I got up from the road and sprinted all the way back to my car. Getting into it, I charged towards the same direction where Cherry's car went.... I kept on driving for 15 minutes, but I didn't see Cherry's car. Realizing that I may have taken the wrong road somewhere and completely missed her path, I stopped. As my attempt to stop Cherry went vain, I turned devastated and screamed my lungs out.

With a heavy heart, I reached the island and dialed Cherry from Aston's mobile. But she rejected my call. Painfully, I called her once again. This time I heard her mobile was switched off. Following these failed efforts, Aston texted Cherry from his social media platforms. However, we didn't get a reply from her. With Cherry's rejection, I was deeply disturbed....

The past five months of beauty in Cherry's intimacy, now perished with her exit. I couldn't bear Cherry's departure and her absence kept crushing me every second. This felt like a hundred arrows pierced my heart at once. Along with this heartbreak engendered from Cherry's exit, I wasn't able to cope up with my sin towards granny. Blaming myself for her death, I was overwhelmed with guilt. The guilt of granny's demise, and the torment of Cherry's departure, shoved me into deep misery. I couldn't eat. I couldn't sleep. Gah, how could I eat, when I was torn apart by the breakup! How could I sleep, when the intense guilt was destroying me! Recalling Cherry and granny constantly in these gloomy times, I cried for weeks in their thoughts. This showed a deep effect on me physically. My entire body became thin and weak. Dark circles appeared under my eyes. My hair fell out like never before. It seemed like all my handsomeness had melted in this misery.

With this misery decaying me physically and psychologically, I felt dead from inside. I felt I needed a relentless punishment for what I had done to Granny and Cherry. I felt I deserved the pain. So, I took a knife and cut my wrist. Blood began to flow out from my wound. But my agony did not subside with one single cut. Feeling that I deserved more suffering, I made a few more deep cuts over my wrist. Meanwhile, Aston entered the room with breakfast. He was shocked at seeing me lacerating my wrist.

'Oh my god! Joe no, stop it...' Shouting in shock, Aston right away dropped the breakfast plate and rushed to me.

Catching my hand in which the knife was in, he tried to snatch it from me. Infuriated over Aston for doing this, I began my onslaught by striking him all over. Unable to combat this attack, Aston slapped me hard. With this slap, I left the knife to the floor. I didn't counter Aston anymore and broke down into tears. Taking control over me and the situation, Aston hurriedly picked up a shirt from the wardrobe and tightly placed it over my wounds. This made the bleeding stop. He then called my doctor.

Doctor arrived and treated my hand. Knowing the cause of why I imposed self-harm, he prescribed antidepressants. Doctor may have thought he could eliminate my misery by giving me these medications. But no antidepressant drugs could heal the wounds that happened to my heart and those wounds continued to show their effect on me....

One night, I ran away from the island and reached granny's grave. Accusing myself of her death, I collapsed beside her grave and wept in agony. After some time, Aston located me and dragged me back to the island.

Alongside the guilt, I was unable to digest Cherry's absence and kept on grieving for her. Aston was worried about my condition as I was drowning in more distress day by day. He texted Cherry but there was no response from her side. So Aston visited Cherry's nursery to find any clues about her. There, he came to know that Cherry had relocated to Agra and given her nursery for lease.

How could I constrain myself to the island after knowing where Cherry is! I felt that if I didn't try to reach Cherry by surrendering to my fears, I could never forgive myself. I've committed a sin and I need to clean it up. I don't have any other way. I had to decide between my fears or Cherry. I chose Cherry. I had to decide whether I should die in this misery or to have a beautiful life with Cherry. I chose Cherry. With the excruciating guilt of granny's sin, and in hope of bringing Cherry back into my life, I left for Agra in my private jet.

BACK TO MY JOURNEY

After landing in Agra, I tried every possible option to reach Cherry but couldn't. I then understood my change could patch up her shattered heart and this would be the only way to reach her. To convince Cherry that I was willing to change, I planned a concert. But I failed in that concert by succumbing to my fears. And now, I was on my way to Thenzawl to prove my change to Cherry by getting that plant myself.

My journey in this Northeastern part of India, felt so lovely. The greenery, the tea gardens, and the rolling hills all around pleased my eye. The curvy road on which I was travelling was going through the rolling hills by penetrating the mild fog. While driving on that road from the middle of those tea gardens, the sight around me looked so splendid. As the orange rays of morning sun falling on those tea gardens, leaves of the tea plants were gleaming in golden beige tone. Impressing my eyes even further, warm orange rays of morning sun mingled with the whitish fog and turned into peach colour. Beneath that fog, tea gardens which were glimmering in golden beige tone on those rolling hills seemed like the soft skin of a seductive naked woman who was covering her nudity with a transparent veil. My mind, which was blindly believing that there was no other place on this planet which could beat my island in terms of beauty, changed its opinion straightaway by seeing this spectacular place.

Driving in this northeastern part of India felt so different from the rest of the country. Every place which I passed through in this nation was fully packed with hordes. But here, it was different. Though I could spot a few village people working here and there in those tea gardens, nature was the dominating aspect over the people here. I felt so grateful to this part of the world due to its breathtaking beauty. Though I previously heard about the diversity of this country, I was shocked by seeing it in person. . . 'From glorifying history of Agra to the untidy roads of villages. From dusty congested cities to breathtaking beauty of tea garden valleys in the northeast, showed me the diverse nature of this vast country'. . .

After driving for about an hour, fuel gauge indicated low fuel level. On the way, I saw a fuel station. I drove my car into that fuel station and stopped at the diesel dispenser. Without getting down from the car, I pulled down my window just a bit (to not reveal my entire face) and asked the staff person to fill up the whole tank in a jittery state. While he started to fill my tank, an ice cream van which was before me, completed to fill its fuel and moved forward. At this time, just in front of the fuel station, I spotted a boy of roughly 5 years old collecting empty water bottles from the roadside dump. Appearance of that boy seemed scruffy. His face and hair were filled with dirt. His clothes were untidy along with patches all over. His feet were bare and muddy. Seeing him, I turned so disgusted, and a vomiting sensation triggered in me instantly. 'How the heck such people exist???' I felt within me, by controlling my nausea. . . During this time, I didn't even expect that this poverty-stricken boy was going to give me great enlightenment and open up a new dimension in my upcoming journey. . .

While putting those collected water bottles into a large garbage bag, that boy saw the ice cream van heading out from the fuel station. Immediately, he stopped his chore and ran to that van. Reaching near to it, he kept gazing at that van by licking his lips, probably with a desire to have an ice cream. But that van passed by him, and his face turned dejected. It was obvious to me that this poor kid didn't have any money to buy an ice-cream, and I thought no one would fulfill his desire now. But I was wrong. The van which passed him, stopped a few feet away and a lady stepped down from it. She opened the back door of that van and picked up an ice cream cone from the freezer, and gave it to that boy with a hearty smile. Then she left that place in her van. That little boy's face which was filled with dejection, now lit up with ecstasy with ice cream in his hand. Noticing this kind of joyful excitement in his face, my aversion on him was wiped out and I kept staring at him in a mesmerized state without even blinking my eyes. Removing the cover of that ice cream cone, that kid began to eat it with great happiness. This happiness appeared so prominent by completely outshining the dirt on his face. Watching him, my heart was submerged in pleasure and my eyes turned wet. I didn't know why! But it felt so nice to see that little boy's face which was filled with joy. I wondered how could an incident that was not at all related to me, make me feel so good? And that kid's blissful face which was pleasing my heart stood as an answer to this question. I kept watching him until he finished eating the ice cream and left from that place. After his exit, I question myself, 'Even that kid who's living in such horrible poverty, has joyfulness in his face. Though being a billionaire, have I ever seen happiness on my face???' I was fucked up with the answer, and ferreted out the truth that I was the most poorest person on this planet in terms of happiness.... Couple of seconds later, my car's tank got filled. I then paid the money and started from there.

Many gifted aspects in life and billions of wealth, never gave me any pleasure. But one little kid who doesn't even have good clothes to wear, generated sheer delight in me. 'Why?' I wondered!

'It's because of witnessing bliss on his face. Yes! A blissful face, which I had never seen in me or in any one else since the years.' I realized instantaneously.

Even though I left that place and went many miles forward, the joyful image of that kid didn't leave me. I got the feeling that I have seen something significant. After Cherry's beautiful eyes, it's this little kid who impacted me to this level. So I felt it was worth to capture that joy on his face. Immediately, I stopped the car to the roadside. Picking up the sketchbook from my bag, I started sketching the blissful face of that kid when he received ice cream from that lady....

After 50 minutes of effort, I completed the sketch. Somehow his face came out in full joyful mode, exactly as I had seen. With this outcome, I got a feeling that I had achieved a great victory, because this was the only happy face which I had successfully portrayed in my entire life. I thought of how I triumphantly depicted the joyful face now. And I figured out that it happened only because of experiencing joyful emotion directly in person, which indeed moved me to successfully portray the joy in this sketch.

After seeing a blissful face and drawing it victoriously, my view over this journey changed completely. I felt that this journey couldn't be limited only to getting that plant. I felt that this journey is a great opportunity to see more joyfulness around, which could help me in depicting genuine joy in my painting as well. With this self-realization, I began to drive forward....

After an hour of drive, my eyes caught an attractive scene. Immediately I hit the brakes and the car stopped. Since beginning this journey, I never stopped the car except when I was tired or to refuel. But now, without any of these reasons I stopped the car. That was because I saw a group of little children playing on the embankment of roadside rice farms, while their elders engaged with chores in those farms. These kids seemed so pleasing to my eyes, because their faces were filled with delightful smiles and joy. For the past two and half decades, I never saw those many joyful faces together, and I thoroughly enjoyed watching them. After feasting my eyes on those children for a good ten minutes, I started from there since I was still a long way from reaching my destination....

On the way, whenever I got down from the car to get some food or other essentials, I witnessed random acts of love towards me from local villagers and passersby for being a foreigner. Their warm reception made me feel good.... Driving forward, I continued to discover tons of people with joyful faces. Their joyfulness brought great pleasure to me and I captured those faces in my sketchbook. My sketchbook which didn't even have a single happy face until the start of this journey, now was filled with many jolly faces. This happened only because of this journey, and I felt so thankful to it for introducing me to the happiness around. Alongside drawing the joyful faces, I also sketched some stunning sceneries which I found on my way. I was so pleased to witness such fine beauty and joy around and this made me forget my past pains. Throughout my life, I believed that the world was devilish. But this journey proved I was utterly wrong. World had shown me all its demons when I looked at it frightfully. Now, when I see the good in it, the same world is showing me the absolute beauty of it. After decades of darkness, enjoying this beauty around me in the daylight, I kept moving forward....

By 8:30 am the next morning, I entered Mizoram state. What I could see all around in this state was tall mountains and widely spread forests with few villages here and there. Population here seemed so minimal when compared to the rest of other Indian states that I crossed. But I was not so surprised by seeing the low population of this state. What surprised me the most in this part of the country was the people themselves. These people looked like Southeast Asians rather than Indians. Till now, I had no idea that the people here look like this! And I was amazed by learning this fact. These people's faces looked very innocent and genuine without any guile. Utterly disgusted and terrified by seeing wild emotions from the people all my life, it felt good to see these calm and innocent faces in this part of the world.

After 6 hours of drive in this state, I entered Thenzawl town. Following the map directions in the mobile, I moved towards my destination. 15 minutes later, I finally arrived at that nursery after three and half days of long and memorable journey.

I covered my face with hood and stepped down from the car. To my front, there was the nursery garden with a beautiful backdrop of the tall mountain range. The name, 'Green Treasures', was shining with silver letters over the wooden arch of that nursery entrance. I was excited to see the nursery. Alongside this excitement, I was concerned about how I could deal with the people inside! Holding my nerves, I walked into the nursery.

Once I stepped in, I noticed a dozen people scattered across that nursery garden. Seeing them, my nervousness grew higher. I couldn't figure out the staff amongst those people and thought whom should I approach for the plant??? While I was in this agitation, I heard a soft voice from my back saying, 'Hello, welcome....'

Listening to this voice, I turned back and saw a stout man with a welcoming smile. He was in mid 40's, and looked like a typical Mizoram man.

'Tell me... What do you want?' He asked politely.

'Can... can I talk to the nursery owner...' I said nervously.

'Yeah, that's me. How can I help you?'

'I... I learned that this nursery has Diamond of Kinabalu orchid plants. Can I see them?'

'Sure! Please follow me.' He said and walked towards the greenhouse.

I followed him from behind in an edgy state. Entering the green house, we headed towards its right end. Then, slowly, my nose started to sense the lovely, sweet fragrance. This was the same scent which I sensed during the time of my childhood memory, and an excitement kicked in me. As we kept walking forward, that fragrance grew even sweeter. My eyes couldn't control themselves and started searching for that plant before reaching it. Then, about 4-5 meters away from me, I spotted 3 plants having a cluster of flowers on top of them. These were the flowers I was looking for, and my eyes couldn't see anything around, except those flowers.

Reaching those plants, nursery owner said, 'These are the plants you asked for'.

Seeing my desirable flowering plant after months of vigorous search, I felt extremely content. Gently taking a flower into my hand, I sniffed its sweet scent in great pleasure.

Finding the plant I wanted, I decided to buy it. 'What's the cost of the plant?' I asked the nursery owner.

'35 lakh rupees,' he replied.

Without wasting the time, I bought the plant for the price he said. Well, one could think purchasing a plant for 3.5 million rupees is extravagant. But the rarity of this plant, and the importance of its flowers in my painting, make this purchase worth every penny. . .

While packing the plant, nursery owner asked, 'What's your name?'

'Joe...' I replied.

'I am Senna,' he introduced himself.   'Which country are you from?' asked Senna.

'Norway,' I replied.

'Where are you staying in the town?' Senna asked.

'I just arrived here from Delhi for this plant,' I said. I said Delhi because, I didn't want to reveal that I came from Agra, which could tell him about me.

Meanwhile Senna finished packing the plant. Walking back to my car with the plant gave me a real sense of achievement. I never dreamt that I could step out from my confinement and get my desirable needs myself. But today, in the daylight, with some people around me, I stood here with the grand trophy of this plant as a glory over my disabilities. I felt so pleased with what I had achieved. Reaching my car, I kept the plant in and started my return journey to Agra.

LIKE A BIRD

Witnessing happiness and successfully sketching many blissful faces on the way to Thenzawl, I learned that chasing happiness was the only way to depict true joy in my painting. But now, as I begin my return journey, I worried that my fears will confine me to the house without making me to pursue happiness once I reach Agra. I don't want this to happen anymore, and started thinking what to do???

While pondering about this, an exceptional idea popped up in my mind. . . 'Far away from the protective forces who could guard me from all my fears, in the company of my own freedom, how will it be if I stay back here in this beautiful part of the world until I finish my artwork?'. . .

Though this idea appeared to be bold, I felt that this experience will not only help me in chasing happiness for my painting, but also help in reinventing myself by improving me from my fears. Apart from these, I felt that I could grandly prove my change to Cherry if I stay here and complete my painting.

Understanding the significance of this newly emerged thought, I decided to stay back there by renting a house. Though the fears which were rooted deeply in me kept pulling me back, the happiness I was witnessing since the beginning of the journey and all the blissful faces which occupied my sketch book pushed me forward by encouraging me to stay there until I triumphantly complete my painting. Perceiving the good that could happen to me if I stay back here, I called off my return journey to Agra and started searching for a rental house in the outskirts of Thenzawl.

All the vacant houses of the outskirts were very close to one another without any serenity and privacy. I kept on searching, but couldn't find a suitable house. Meanwhile, time turned to late noon. As I failed to find an appropriate house even after hours of search, I was vexed, and I also started feeling hungry. Finding a tea stall on the way, I stopped my car in front of it to have some tea and snacks. When I got down from the car, a stout man who was passing on the road on his bike halted suddenly upon seeing me. I didn't understand why he stopped! And a fear aroused in me instantly. As his face was covered with a helmet, I didn't even get a chance to see who he was! Getting down from the bike, he walked towards me by removing his helmet. Once that helmet came off his head, I came to know that he was Senna. I was shocked to see him here.

'Hey Joe, what are you doing here?' Senna asked in a surprised state after reaching me.

'Just stopped here to have tea. What about you?'

'I have a farming garden in the nearby village. While going there, I spotted you here. I thought you had already left the town.'

'Nope! I... I have decided to stay here for few days,' I said hesitantly.

'Oh, that's cool. There are good hotels back in the town.'

'No no. I don't want to stay in a hotel. I'm intending to rent a house in a calm and peaceful place,' I said, because I cannot stay freely in a hotel due to the constant presence of people over there.

Then, thinking for a while Senna said, 'If you don't mind, can I say something?'

'Yeah....' I granted.

'I have a small farmhouse in my farming garden. I will take you there. And if you like that house, you can stay there.'

Delighted upon hearing this, I agreed to see that house.

After having a cup of tea and some biscuits, we both started to that place. While Senna was going on his bike, I followed him in my car. After driving for about 10 minutes, we crossed a small village and reached a canal. Senna turned his bike on to the bridge which was above that canal. Crossing that bridge, we entered a narrow mud road. Driving forward on that mud road, I saw various fruit gardens with tall mountains behind. In those vastly spread fruit gardens, I noticed a few houses scattered here and there. After 5-6 minutes of drive through this beautiful location, Senna stopped his bike beside a dragon fruit farm and came to me. Seeing him, I dropped the window. Then he pointed his finger towards a small cement house, which was in an open space beside that farm, and said, 'Park the car in front of that house'.

Saying this, he walked into that house. Following his instruction, I parked my car in front of that house. While waiting for Senna who went inside, I casually looked all around that place. Just a few meters to my right, I saw a decent sized house with an orange gutter roof. Thirty meters to my left there was that dragon fruit garden spread in a vast area. Some distance behind that fruit garden, there was a tall mountain range. Clouds were gliding in the skies by skimming the summits of those mountains, which enhanced the beauty of that place even higher. Suddenly, an Asian koel welcomed me by singing a lovely koo koo song from somewhere nearby. With this koel song and the beauty around, that place seemed as the heaven which plunged down directly onto the earth's surface. A moment later, I saw Senna coming out of that cement house with a key in his hand. Along with him, a lady and a cute little boy (of roughly 4 years old) stepped out of that house and stood at its doorstep. Senna walked to me and gestured to get down from the car. When I got down the car, I noticed that the lady was gazing at me with a look of wonder in her face, and that little boy kept staring towards me from behind her.

I felt edgy as they stared at me and I put down my head immediately. Senna asked me to follow him and took me to that gutter roofed house. After entering, he showed all corners of that house to me. Though the house had no luxuries that I needed, I was pleased to see the house in the middle of such beautiful nature, that too with very little people around.

'How's the house?' Senna queried.

'I liked it... How much should I pay to stay here?'

'I have already charged 35 lakh rupees from you. I have to admit that this is a higher price than normal. It's not ethical to expect more from you,' said Senna with gratitude.

'What! Are you sure?' I asked, admiring his frankness.

'Yeah. You said you will be here only for a few days, so it's not a big deal.'

'What about the food? Where can I get some veggies or meat here?' I queried.

'Vendors will come here in auto-rickshaws regularly. You can purchase fruits and vegetables from them. But for meat and other groceries, you have to go downtown.'

'Oh! ok...'

'I will speak to that woman who lives in the out house. She works for me and looks after this farm. If you want any assistance you can ask her, or you can call me,' Senna said by giving his card.

'Sure...' I replied and took that card from him.

'Have a good time here.' Senna wished me.

'Thank you,' I replied.

He then left the house.

With Senna's exit, I called dad and said that I have rented a house in Thenzawl to stay here until finishing my art work. At first, my decision left dad in shock. But then he welcomed my resolution, and wished me to achieve success with my painting. After ending his call, I spent some time in the house and adapted myself to those new surroundings.

At 8:30 pm in the night, I left to the town to buy all the necessary tools and equipment for my painting.... While at the store, I observed a few people with pointed looks at me. I was scared of those people, but decided to ignore them, so that they will mind their own business. Without even looking at them, I quickly picked up all the needed equipment for my painting. I then paid the money and rushed out of that store.

Next morning, a chaotic incident took place between me and that kid who lived in the outhouse.... When I sat down in my bedroom and sketching a thumbnail of Flam farm as a reference to my painting, I noticed that kid peeping into my room from the other side of the window through the tiny curtain gap. With this wild act from him, I sensed that he was so curious about me because I looked like an alien to him, coming into his world from different part of the globe. As he kept peeping at me, I felt uncomfortable and didn't understand how to react! To stop him from further peeping in, I pulled the curtain to the end without leaving any gap for him to see in. After closing that curtain on his face, I thought he will never repeat these kinds of actions again. But the chaos between two of us did not stop there itself....

That evening, when I was slicing mango for my snack, I heard the door knock. Anxiously thinking who was that, I opened the door and saw that kid at my doorstep. He was holding a tiny basket which was filled with guavas. Seeing the basketful of guavas, I thought that his mom or Senna may have sent those fruits with him! While I was in this thought, in a flash he stepped into my house without my invitation and kept that basket on the table. I was perplexed and annoyed with this strange behaviour from him, and waited at the door to close it once he exited the house. But shockingly, he didn't leave the house and kept looking towards the plate which contained the sliced mango pieces. Unable to understand how to tackle this situation, I calmly came back from the main door and continued to slice the mango by glancing at him. While I was cutting the fruit, he kept staring at it with a mouth watering face. Observing this, I thought that he was desiring to have it. So I offered him a piece of mango. Taking that piece to his little hand, he started to eat it by looking at me with a blank expression on his face. A while later, he finished having it and calmly exited the house without even thanking me or even looking at me. While just about to step into his house, he turned back and left a lovely smile at me. With that smile, he then went into his house. His divine smile generated great delight in me, and in all of a sudden, my loathsome opinion over that kid had vanished.

Next day, when I saw that kid, I invited him into my house and gave him the whole bar of Duffy's chocolate to see a smile on his face again. Receiving the chocolate, his face lit up with fascinating joy, significantly higher than I expected. Unwrapping the cover of that chocolate, he started to consume it with great elation. Seeing that elation on his face, a great pleasure kicked in me and my heart was filled with delight. Without even turning my eyes away from him, I kept watching him until he finished eating that chocolate....

Once he finished it, I asked, 'What's your name?'

But he didn't reply anything and kept looking at me in silence. Assuming that the kid didn't get me, I once again asked, 'Name.... Your name...?'

Without replying, he walked off from me and stood at my doorstep. From there, he gestured that he cannot speak. He then wiped the chocolate around his mouth, and with a smiling face he walked to his house.

Knowing that he was dumb, I felt so sorry for his misfortune. Although I could not know that boy's name through his mouth, I later learned that his name was 'Guddu' as his mother called him by this name.

I often offered Duffy's chocolates to Guddu to see his bliss again and again. While he was eating it, I perked up by watching his ecstatic face. After Guddu's exit, I kept capturing those joyful emotions of his face in my sketchbook.

One day, when I gave my little friend a chocolate, he ate it as usual. But after finishing that chocolate, he kept looking at me. I was puzzled and remained silent by gazing at him. Then, he slowly kept his hand in his pocket. Seeing this, a curiosity was raised in me. A second later, he took out closed palm from his pocket. Keeping that closed palm up towards me, he slowly opened it with a lovely smile on his face. Inside his little palm, I saw a small chocolate candy. I suddenly recalled my mom who used to do the same. And this instinctively brought tears in my eyes. Feeling absolute pleasure, I knelt down at Guddu and picked that chocolate by fondly pampering his cheek. This beautiful incident with Guddu, really made my day.

From the next day, he continued to offer me chocolate candy whenever he visited me. Without consuming those chocolates, I kept collecting them in a box. I did this because those chocolates were a symbolism of my great times with my little friend. So, I kept them as trophies of my sweet memories with him.

As days passed by, we both used to be together for the majority of the day and have some lovely times by playing silly games, fishing in the nearby pond, roaming across the farming garden and plucking the fruits, and collecting the ground pigments for making paints. The days kept passing with no conversation between us. But our hearts had developed a perfect rapport and kicked off to interact with one another with exquisite emotions, which felt more heartwarming than having a normal chat.

One late afternoon.... As I already drew numerous joyful sketches successfully, I sat down to sketch my childhood memory. On the halfway to my sketch, I felt that it was not appearing so satisfactory in matching the intensity of my laughs and happiness of my memory. Though the sketch was not turning out as I desired, I finished it without leaving in the middle. The result seemed better than all of my previous childhood sketches, but not good enough to impel me to start my painting. It was a mixed bag of feelings for me. I felt good to see improvement in extracting the joy on my childhood face. At the same time, I felt bad for still being unable to match up to the joy of my childhood memory.

When I was submerged in these mixed feelings, my ears started to catch up to the cheerful laughs of kids from outside. To see what was going on, I walked to the hall and peeped out through the window. In the open area in front of my house, I saw Guddu playing cricket with five other kids (who were about 5-6 years old). Their game of cricket seemed totally different from the actual cricket. The bat which they were using was made up of dried coconut branch with all its leaves peeled off. They placed a steel oil tin in the place of stumps. The ball which they were playing with was a blue rubber one. It felt so funny to see this kind of cricket. I laughed inward wondering, 'Can the cricket be played in this manner also!!!' Though the kind of sport which they were playing felt so immature and funny, on the other side of the coin, I could see the joy and enjoyment in the faces of those kids while playing that silly village cricket. I was so pleased by witnessing the good times which these kids were blessed with. I watched them until they were forcibly dispersed by their parents when the sky started to turn dark.

Next evening, those kids started playing cricket outside of my house once again. Watching them playing, my heart desired to go out and play with them. But I did not understand how to go and mingle with those kids by myself! So, without stepping out, I constrained myself behind the walls of my hall and kept watching them through the window. An hour later, sky started to turn dark and the kids faced difficulty in facing the ball. Even the small incandescent bulb which was at the doorstep of that outhouse, didn't provide enough light for them. Along with this difficulty, another hurdle arose for those kids in the form of their parents. As the sky became dark, Guddu's mother came and interrupted the play and made those kids disperse. While walking back to their homes, the faces of those kids were filled with dejection. It felt so bad for me to see their glum little faces which were filled with great joy until a while ago. With their exit, that place turned dead silent without any laughs and cheerful shrieks....

Even on the next day, parents interrupted the kids' play once the sky turned dark. Observing the sadness in their faces while leaving the place, I became upset. Feeling for them, I started to think, what can make them play for as long as they wanted? Then, I got an idea which could solve those kids' problem. Straightaway, I out plugged the fluorescent lights from the kitchen and the hall. I then stepped out and fixed them to the front wall of my house. After giving the connection, I switched on the lights. Shoving darkness to all the corners, that open area in front of my house turned bright in the glow of those two fluorescent tubes. By arranging this light setup, I felt that the kids could play for as long as they wished. . . 'There was a self-interest in doing this. I intended that the death of light should not interrupt those little kids' game and their happiness anymore. So that I can enjoy watching them playing merrily'. . .

When the next time those kids came together and playing cricket, light died out same as the previous days, and kids felt trouble facing the ball. Noticing this, I stepped out of the house and switched on those lights. Suddenly the darkness of that area filled up with bright light. Seeing the light in that place, those kids were greatly thrilled. Since I was at the switchboard which was outside of my doorstep, they all gazed at me in elation. Seeing their elated faces, my heart was filled with instinctive pleasure. All the hard work that went into fixing those lights, now received a great reward by seeing the bliss on their faces. Meanwhile, Guddu's mother came out to disperse them. But because of having a good amount of light, those kids convinced her to play for some more time and sent her off. Then, they continued to play, and I stood at my doorstep watching them playing....

A while later, an unexpected event occurred. Kid who was batting, hit the ball hard. The ball smashed one of my house's window and fell inside. Suddenly, all their innocent faces turned frightened by looking at me. They might have thought that I may rebuke them for breaking the window glass. Seeing this fright in those little faces, I felt very odd. To fill up the joy in their faces again, I went inside my house and collected the ball. I then came out and offered it to Guddu with a smile on my face. Seeing my smile, Guddu's gloomy face turned relieved, and subsequently he grinned at me in reply. As I was offering him the ball, I thought that he will take it from my hand. But instead of taking the ball, he caught my hand in which the ball was in.

He then took me to his friends and offered the bat for me to play. . . 'I thought it's the gratitude towards me for not rebuking them, and for arranging lights for them to play'. . . I couldn't believe my luck, as my craving for playing with them came true finally due to this initiative from Guddu. I felt a bit tense but took that bat into my hand hesitantly and started playing with them. We laughed, we yelled in joy, we mocked each other when we failed to hit or catch the ball. Although playing this silly village cricket and that too with six year old kids felt so childish, the delight which I gained through this time was immeasurable. As long as I was in the house, I had only seen the joy on those kids' faces. But now, I could feel that joy inside me while playing with them. That's when for the first time, I understood the difference between watching the joy from the walls of my confinement and taking part in it directly. My thirty-one years of age had reduced to six. I kicked my fears aside. I didn't bother about anything and enjoyed this precious time wholeheartedly. It was a beautiful experience of my life, which I will never forget.

We played until we got tired. Then we returned home. Though those children went away from me, the joy which they gave didn't leave me. That day had ended with great delight.

Next day.... Craving to have some joy again, I waited for those kids' arrival. When the time turned to late noon, they all gathered in front of my house. Seeing them, I stepped out myself directly, without getting any call from them. We all had a blast of time by playing hide and seek in the fruit garden, and following this, we played our silly village cricket with the iconic coconut branch.

As the days went by, I thoroughly enjoyed my time with these kids, and they did the same with me. Till a few days ago, Guddu was my only friend. But now I had five others, they were Sanju, Hminga, Viru, Cyril and Shiva. Spending time with these little buddies gave me the joy I missed and made me experience the beauty of childhood. I was so pleased to have such blissful times in their amity. . . 'It felt like time had pity on my past and gave me a chance to have my childhood again, this time in a cheerful manner'. . . All the previous cravings of my childhood which were constrained within the walls of my classroom and mansion, now got fulfilled in the company of these kids. With these good times, I felt happy from inside and the distress of my past abated due to this happiness. No medication gave me relief from my agonies, but this happiness eventually did.

During nights, I often sketched the joy I noticed on the faces of my little friends. In addition to drawing these, I also sketched the beautiful moments that took place between us.

After drawing many blissful faces, one fine day I decided to give it a try in making my Childhood sketch again. After 4 hours of vigorous effort, I finally succeeded in sketching the joy in my childhood face, exactly matching the laughs and happiness of my memory. Maybe this had happened due to the joy which I can feel inside of me now, and because of the joy I was witnessing around me. My laugh in this sketch told the true meaning of happiness. My eyes in the sketch stood as a pinnacle of joy. I said thanks to myself for drawing the sketches of Cherry's eyes in the past, and for observing the joyful emotions in the eyes of my little friends which made this happen. With the triumphant result of this sketch, I felt I had achieved a massive victory in my life.

This successful outcome of the sketch propelled me to start my painting. I carefully extracted the fragrance from Diamond of Kinabalu orchid flowers into oil. Then, I blended that fragrant oil with ground pigments and veg purees and prepared the palette. Using these purees, I started to paint by putting that newly drawn sketch as a reference.

As days kept passing, I engaged myself with the painting. During leisure times, Guddu and I continued to hang out with each other. He never stopped giving me chocolate candy. And the chocolates in that box kept on increasing day by day, just like my happiness. In the late noons, upon completion of their school, our other five friends used to join Guddu and me. After having some wonderful time with them, I used to sit with my painting until late at night.

The same routine had continued for the next 10 days. But then, fate showed its cruelty over me again....

Spring had finished and summer began. With this summer, schools got a break. I thought I could have an awesome time with my buddies all day due to the summer break. But that didn't happen because all my friends went to other places to enjoy their vacation. Finally, there were only two of us left behind, Guddu and I. Front yard of my house which was filled with the joyful laughs and silly games previously, now turned silent....

In the absence of my friends, I mostly concentrated my evening time on painting. And during the day, Guddu provided me good company. We both done birding in the farming gardens, played cricket in the front yard, and made some colours for my painting. When my days were moving in a decent manner, I got another blow. Guddu started to go downtown along with his mother, who committed to take part in Senna's nursery works. The only times when I could see Guddu was during mornings when he was heading out to the town and in the nights after returning home. With no one around me, my world was filled with emptiness. I felt this loneliness so heavy. For the first time in my life, I noticed a strange change in me that I couldn't tolerate the loneliness in which I spent all my life. To counter this solitude, I assigned the majority of my time to painting. Along with this, I had also dedicated some time to record specific sounds relating to the scene in my painting. Blowing wind, moving grass, and my footsteps in the grass (which I could use while chasing butterflies), were some of the sounds I had recorded. Whenever I took some break from painting, I sat alone on the doorstep of my house and recalled all the precious memories that I spent with my little friends in the front yard. An entire week had passed in this manner. And in all these days, I successfully managed to turn out my painting exactly as desired.

One night.... Around 8:30 pm, nature started to show its brutality with boisterous winds and heavy rain. Due to this violent weather, power went off and interrupted me from painting. After an hour of ravaging storms, nature calmed down but the power didn't come. Seeing that there would be no electricity throughout the night and I couldn't continue my painting, I went to bed. A while later, when I was about to sleep, I heard the prolonged sound of door bangs along with a faint cry. Listening to this, my sleep got disrupted and I woke up from the bed. I was baffled, and moreover tensed, by listening to the door bang and a cry during the time of late night. Putting on the emergency light, I walked to the door with a series of bad thoughts running through my mind. Once I reached the door and opened it, I saw Guddu's mother in devastating sob telling me something. As I didn't know her language, I didn't get what she was saying!!! But due to her sob, I sensed something went horribly wrong. My tense turned to fright. She caught my hand and took me into the outhouse. Inside the house, I saw Guddu laying on the floor mattress. Though his mom was trying to wake him up in tears, he was not responding to her. His upper eyelids were dropped. There was only a slight moment in his head and hands. It looked like he was semi paralyzed. I was terrified and heartbroken by seeing this. It felt that all the joyfulness which Guddu induced in my life, was at the verge of great threat along with him. Then, in the dim glow of my emergency light, I saw two puncture wound marks on his left arm with swelling around it. Noticing this, I doubted that he may have been bit by some snake. I immediately decided to take Guddu to the hospital. I rushed to my house and picked up the car key. I took Guddu into my arms and put him in the back seat of my car. Following the directions of Guddu's mother who was in the back seat, I drove the car towards the hospital.

When we were about to reach the hospital, I saw a huge tree that had collapsed in the middle of the road due to the storm. The hospital was in sight at around 300 meters away from me. But to reach it, the hurdle which stopping us was the fallen tree which blocked the road completely, and a few dozens of bikers and motorists were jammed on either side of that tree. There were some workmen working to clear up the tree, but it looked like it would take a long time for them to do so. I didn't understand what to do by seeing those people in front of me. I was sunk in absolute terror. The entire scenario seemed somewhat resembling the granny's incident. While I was in this terror-stricken mode, the devastating anguish of a mother who was in my back seat, and her child who was fighting for life, forced me to do something. Since there was no chance to drive forward, taking Guddu to hospital on foot seemed the only possible way. So I put the car to the roadside and got down. Warning myself that I couldn't forgive myself if I end up committing another clanger, I took Guddu to my arms and I started to dash towards the hospital. All the bikers and the motorists looked back towards me and kept gazing at me with stunned faces. Observing all their pointed looks at me, panic kicked in me and I stood still by stopping. My heart, which was already beating fast, now began to beat tremendously faster. My body started to shiver. I was filled with sweat. I felt nausea and dizziness. My panicking mind was stuck with the thought of, 'This will be another disaster'.

'No... Not again. I should not let it happen this time....' I strongly said to myself, and decided to face this difficulty at any cost.

Gathering all my courage and strength, I began to rush forward through those bikers and motorists. I could see that all those people were looking at me. I could feel that I was utterly crushed by my fears. But saying to myself that, 'I couldn't leave my little friend and his mother helplessly on the road by succumbing to my fears again', I pushed myself further by fighting against my fears and reached that fallen tree. With the help of those workmen who were clearing that tree, we managed to climb it and reached the other side of the tree. Rushing through the vehicles which were present on the other side of that tree, we finally reached the hospital.

As soon as we entered the hospital, nursing staff took Guddu into the emergency ward. I was so worried about his condition. In addition to this, people's presence around me and the panic that was engendered on the way to hospital, put me in extreme anxious mode. Though I was anxious, I stood by Guddu's mother.

Doctor examined Guddu and questioned his mother about the detailed history and concluded that he was bitten by a neurotoxic snake. Immediately, IV cannula was secured to Guddu and anti-snake venom treatment was started. Some blood tests were performed on Guddu. Reading the test reports, doctor said that Guddu's condition is critical.

Hospital staff asked to pay the deposit for the treatment. While paying money, I saw Guddu's mother pleading with the cashier at the cash counter. Understanding that something was wrong, I went there and asked the cashier, 'What's the problem???'

'She only had 10 thousand rupees. For the tests done and as deposit fee, she needs to pay 1 lakh rupees,' replied the cashier.

Knowing that she was short of money, I paid the remaining 90 thousand rupees. Guddu is my dearest friend and it's my responsibility to pay when his mom can't afford the treatment for him. With the payment done, treatment to Guddu was continued.... Throughout the night Guddu was in the ICU. His mother and I spent the whole night in the hospital with severe tension over his condition.

At 12 noon, doctor said that Guddu was responding well to the treatment and is out of danger and he will be shifted to the room in 12-24 hours. Hearing this good news, I was mighty relieved. Deeply dented with granny's tragedy, my involvement in saving Guddu made me very happy. While I was proud of what I did, Guddu's mom came to me and broke down in joyful tears by joining both of her hands at me. She started saying something to me in an extremely thankful state. Although I didn't understand what she was saying, I clearly felt deep gratitude towards me in her face. . . 'As they say, emotion doesn't need any language to convey its meaning. And now, in my case, that's proven to be absolutely true'. . . By beholding such a soul-stirring emotion in a mother's face, great euphoria generated in me. This high felt much stronger than the high I got by abusing drugs. My eyes turned wet with this enormous pleasure. I felt very pleased. Completely overwhelmed in this euphoric trance, I didn't even speak a single word to her, and walked off from there with happy tears oozing from my eyes.

I don't know exactly why I walked off from there! Maybe, it was because I wanted to hide my emotions and happy tears from Guddu's mother. Carrying that happiness within me, I reached the hospital lounge. Though I could see people over there fixedly looking towards me, I continued to walk forward without even caring about their presence. The people who made me atrociously frightened all my life, now don't even cause a tiny turbulence in me. . . 'That's maybe due to the trance that I was put into, which sedated my brain from worrying about those people'. . . Holding my emotions, I got into my car and drove all the way back home.

Reaching home, I slammed the door and leaned against it. My inwardly concealed delight until now, exploded like an atomic bomb at once, and I burst out weeping in that prodigious pleasure behind the closed doors of my house. . . 'Witnessing such a heart stirring emotion in a mother, and feeling so content for contributing in saving her son's life, might have made me exhilarated to this level!' . . .

Few minutes later.... I returned to the normal state from that jubilant outburst. But my heart still carried on with immense happiness for lending a helping hand in saving Guddu. For the past few days, I thought that one could experience happiness only by taking part in the joyful events. But now, the satisfaction of being involved in saving a life, and witnessing a mother's gratitude, showed me a new dimension of happiness. The happiness which I felt today was much stronger than all the glad times I had with those kids previously. Guddu's episode made me learn that happiness isn't only confined to joyful times of life, one can achieve it by helping others, getting self-satisfaction, and through many deep emotions which can stir souls, 'Same like Guddu's mother did to me today'.

Overwhelmed with this great happiness, I sat down to paint. I vigorously worked on my painting in the company of my happiness.... Finally, after three hours of effort, I completed the painting. Bliss on my childhood face came out same like in that reference sketch which I drew just before starting this painting. Though I succeeded in depicting the joy on my childhood face, I sensed that there was some kind of flaw in the overall scene of the painting.

I contemplated what could be that flaw, but failed to discover it. I was frustrated. Despite the anger overflowing in me, restraining myself I decided to think calmly about where the mistake had been made. With a cup of tea, I sat on the doorstep of my house. Sipping tea in the lovely late noon's atmosphere, I went on to think what went wrong in the painting? After a while of pondering, I realized that the scene in my painting was a bit dark compared to the late noon's light outside. I immediately went inside and looked at my painting. It seemed dim, the same as I felt. . . 'Having been in the dark for so many years, I may have failed to bring the right amount of light in my painting. Damn! Darkness in my life had taken a toll on my painting as well.' I comprehended. . .

Discovering that the poorly lit scene is letting down the painting, I sat down to fix it. I worked hard for an hour and amplified the light in the scene, but the painting still looked ill-lit. I was disappointed by the result. I started to think how could I get the right amount of light in my painting? When I was thinking about this, my mind came up with an idea which was suggested by Cherry previously. The thought was to go and do painting in the outdoors. 'Yes... Coming out and pursuing happiness made me successfully depict the joy in my painting. The same way if I did the painting in outdoors by studying the light, I could definitely bring out the proper amount of lighting in my painting,' I said to myself.

Strongly believing that there would be a definite success with outdoor sessions, I headed out to paint although I was being pulled down by my fears.

While driving through the outskirts of Thenzawl in search of the right place, I spotted a beautiful grassland which was surrounded by tall mountains on either side. This place reminded me of the vicinities of Flam farm and I stopped the car. Feeling that I found the right place, I went to that grassland and set up the canvas to the easel. Studying the brightness, mood, tones and shades of that location under the light of late noon sun, I started to mend the scene in my painting. I worked for thirty minutes. Then, light subsided over that location and I returned home.

From the next day, around 4:00 pm, I used to go to that place and carry on to mend my painting under the light of the late noon sun. I selected this particular time because the scene in my painting requires late noon's tone and mood as my childhood memory happened during the exact same time.

While I was outdoors, in addition to painting, I began to study the world which was interlinked with tons of emotions from greatest joy to deep misery. People who shared their happiness together, stayed together with each other in times of distress as well. With all these, the world around me seemed to be perfectly balanced with one another. I started to connect the dots between people, that a person's happiness was indefinitely bounded with another's. Joy was multiplied when shared and distress can be subdued in the company of others. I found the true meaning of life with these outdoor painting sessions.

I noticed the drastic change in my painting because of these outdoor sessions. Now, the painting looked brighter than before. This brightness completely wiped out the dullness in the scene. Light in my childhood eyes increased. Rays of the sun fell on my little cheeks with full intensity. Redness on those cute little cheeks was clearly visible in that bright sunlight which enhanced the beauty even more in my joyful face. With the increased brightness, overall scene clearly showed the depth, softly separating the character from the background. With these modifications, painting seemed quite beautiful.

On the eleventh day of my outdoor session, I concluded the final details of my painting. I was overwhelmed with contentment by the way how painting had turned out. This artwork portrayed my joyous emotion in full detail and exactly as it happened. Diamond of Kinabalu orchid's sweet fragrance which was ingrained into the fibres of the canvas, played a crucial role by defining the smell of the background location. More importantly, this fragrance defined my sense of smell which was one of the main factor of my pleasant mood in the time of the memory. After so many months of failed attempts and vigorous efforts, finally the result came out as wished. I was extremely happy with the successful outcome of my painting. With the pleasure of successfully completing the painting, I left for home.

When I entered the house and opened my bedroom door, I was greeted warmly by my sketchbook and chocolate candies which were on the dressing table. I took the sketch book to my hand and started going through each page. Joyful sketches in my sketchbook, and the chocolates given by Guddu reminded me of all the happy times of my recent days. Remembering those beautiful days, I found that my happiness was not just constrained to my childhood memory because I experienced joy every minute since I started my journey to Thenzawl. I was so delighted to obtain happiness after two and half decades of profound distress. While I was overwhelmed with great contentment for victoriously completing the painting and obtaining joy in my life, I looked into the dressing table's mirror by chance while putting the sketchbook back on it. Though I was so happy inside, I noticed that the happiness which was within me was not reflecting on my face. Gazing at my face in that mirror, I contemplated what was the reason for the lack of happiness on my face? Then, I found that my gloomy appearance was concealing the joy in my face. . . 'Damn! Since my face is buried with messy hair and beard, how can it display happiness?' I said to myself. . .

Unable to accept this gloomy disguise, I took it off, to see my happiness in full form beneath it. I then looked into the mirror. Happiness which concealed behind my disguise, now appeared in full scale on my face in this trimmed look. My face that always looked dejected was now glowing, full of joy. I could not believe what I was seeing. It felt like a dream. Unable to restrain myself by witnessing the immense amount of happiness on my face, I leaned my forehead against the mirror and burst into joyful tears. As my t-shirt was unbuttoned, I saw the broken winged bird tattoo on my chest reflecting in the mirror. When I was experiencing happiness in my life and on my face, I could not accept this disturbing tattoo as it was describing the perished freedom and happiness of my life. I thought of what to do with this tattoo??? I then got an amazing idea. Immediately, I took off my shirt. Grabbing the sketch pen from my painting kit, I modified the broken wings and made that tattoo look like a bird flying in the skies with wings outstretched. This temporarily altered tattoo, gloriously described the newborn happiness and freedom in my life. As soon as I finished the tattoo, I started hearing chirping of birds from outside. Listening to those chirping birds, I could not control myself as I finally saw joy on my face and had happiness in my life, just like those birds. Since many years, I have desired freedom and happiness in my life, just like birds. As this dream came true now, I rushed out of the house in great elation to proudly announce this achievement to my feathery friends. I reached the dragon fruit garden from where I could hear those chirps. I spotted some birds flying around that garden. Alongside these birds, I saw a sedge of cranes flying back to their homes in the orange evening sky. Seeing birds all around and up in the skies, I plummeted down to my knees in exultation. Proudly showing the newly modified tattoo over my bare chest up towards those flying birds, I shouted-out, "Hooooo.... I have happiness in my life same as you now.... Come ooon.... Look down at me and see the joy on my face.... Hooooooooo...." Announcing this, I cried like nuts in jubilation.

As I could see happiness on my face now, I felt that this newfound emotion should not be concealed. So I decided to keep this original look without covering my face with any disguise.

I turned eager to convey my success in painting to Cherry and decided to leave for Agra the next morning. I carefully packed my painting, Diamond of Kinabalu orchid plant, those chocolate candies, and my sketchbook. When I started to Thenzawl, I had nothing but a bagful of clothes. But now while going from here, I'm taking all these valuable things with me along with many memorable moments. Coming to Thenzawl and staying here changed my life completely. . . 'On the night before departing to Thenzawl, I was determined to make dad proud. Today, if he knew what I achieved in my life, he will be extremely content for me,' I said to myself. . .   Once I finished packing my stuff, I went to bed.

I woke up early in the morning and loaded all my stuff into the car. I then waited for Guddu's wake up to inform my departure. I feared how Guddu and his mom would react by seeing me as I changed to my popular look now! Though I could simply hide my identity as before, I felt that at least in the time of my departure, I should not fool Guddu by hiding who I am....

After 10 minutes, light was turned on in the outhouse. This announced their wake up. I locked the house and went to the outhouse in an edgy state. Standing at its doorstep, I held my nerve and called, 'Guddu...'

With my call, Guddu and his mom came out. As soon as they saw me, their faces turned baffled. Apart from bafflement, they neither reacted wildly nor excitedly by seeing me in my original form. This made me understand that they didn't know about me, that's why there was no excitement in them. I was surprised to learn this fact. 'Because of living in a remote area of this world and not knowing anything about English music or language, they may not know me,' I thought to myself.

Guddu and his mom kept on looking at me in the same baffled state. I thought that they had been perplexed for suddenly seeing me in this trimmed look. I felt good for revealing my original face to my buddy at last.

Offering the house keys to Guddu's mom, I said, 'I'm leaving. It's too early in the morning to call Senna. I will inform this to him in a couple of hours. Here's the keys'.

Though she didn't know English, the keys which I was offering made her understand that I was leaving. She smiled at me and took the keys.

Then, looking at Guddu I said 'Bye' to him. Listening this, Guddu's face turned glum. In dejection, he rushed into his house. I didn't understand why he went inside! After a while, he came out and offered a chocolate candy to me for one last time. This warm act from Guddu made me quite emotional. My eyes were filled with tears. Controlling myself and the tears, I took the chocolate from him. Then Guddu hugged me. In presence of his mom, his hug made me feel awkward. Despite feeling awkwardness, I hugged Guddu in response.

After this emotional goodbye from Guddu, I got into my car and started it. Guddu's mom gestured 'Bye' by wagging her hand at me. But there was no such gesture from Guddu. He kept staring at me in a saddened mood by holding his mom from behind. It felt so heavy for me to leave Guddu and that beautiful place. But I had to. Looking fixedly at Guddu, I left from there with a heavy heart.

BACK TO AGRA

After reaching Agra, through Aston's email, I posted a photograph of my painting to Cherry's email and informed her that I successfully completed this artwork by staying in Thenzawl.... Then I decided to give my personal interview to the local news channel. Well! One could think why to give an interview? Because I was intending to dedicate something big to Cherry, which I didn't want to mention simply to her in that email. . . One can express a doubt of why I posted an email to Cherry, instead of mentioning my triumph in painting directly through this interview!!! As I kept my painting skill secret from the world, I didn't want to reveal it publicly through the interview. So, this is the reason I sent an email to Cherry, intimating my success in painting only to her. . .

An hour later.... Aston arranged my interview with a local news channel. A lady reporter, camera man, and I sat in the hall of my house, and the interview kicked off.

'Hi.... This is Divya Bhargav. Today we got an opportunity which no media house in this world has gotten till now. It is a great privilege and pleasure for me to have an interview with the legend himself. He is a person who needs no introduction, and here he is. Hello Edward, welcome to my interview....' That reporter introduced me with these praising words.

As this was my first ever interview, and as it was streaming live, I felt so nervous. In this anxious state, I left a forced smile at that reporter in reply to her warm introduction.

'So Edward... We are very eager to know why this interview is being held?'

'Because I... I want to announce a special thing to the dearest person of my life,' I said edgily, stammering.

'Oh! Who is that person? And what is that?' Reporter asked in excitement.

In the same nervousness, I said, 'When.... when I had been vexed in failing to make a song that fulfilled my potential, there was one person who filled enough inspiration in me and made it happen. That person was none other than Cherry. This song was initially made to be dedicated solely to her. But she desired that this song should reach as big a crowd as possible. So I am releasing it as per her wish. The song will be available in the web from this evening. I want to make this known to Cherry and everyone through this interview'.

'Wow! That's great. I hope this song will rock the world just like your previous songs,' said that reporter.   She then excitedly asked, 'Edward... since you have announced that concert for Cherry, there was a huge buzz going over her. Who is she? People desperately want to know about her'.

'I am sorry. I don't want to reveal anything about Cherry publicly.' I refused the reporter's request considering Cherry's privacy.

'It's ok....' She whispered disappointingly.   She then asked, 'You took more than two and half years of gap to come up with a song. Can we expect the next one soon???'

'I hope so....' I replied cleverly, without hinting that I had already quit my career. . . My intention was still clear. I don't want to resume my music career because it would only increase my popularity. I wanted to live a peaceful life without any mess, doing music only for myself. I don't want to raise a storm in public by announcing that I terminated my career. So let the world continue to assume that I will come up with another album soon, which I may never do so. . .

After finishing the interview, while taking my autograph, the cameraman questioned me, 'I didn't understand one thing Edward! Why are you releasing the song for Cherry 2 months after failing in that concert??? If you really want to impress her, it would be so good if you did this right after that failure event'.

There was a significant reason to release this song now, and I don't want to share this reason with anyone. So to get away from his question, I simply said, 'I didn't get this idea back then'.

I did not give that reason to him because I felt that this world doesn't need to know about it. But I believed that Cherry could definitely understand why I'm releasing this song now. My intention was not to impress her. My intention was to honour her. Because I had realized how my life had changed because of Cherry.

After signing my autograph to that cameraman and reporter, I started walking back to my room by recalling the momentous event which had changed everything in my life. . . "A message from Cherry". . .

MESSAGE FROM CHERRY

On the night of that failed concert, when I was wreaking havoc in my room and as the hand gun fell down from the broken wooden drawer, I took that gun and kept it to my head. When I was just about to pull its trigger, dad rushed into my room and shoved the gun away from me. . . He might have come in because of hearing those smashing sounds from my room. If he had entered my room even a second late, that was the end of me. . .

While dad was trying to calm me down, Aston brought me a gift box and mentioned that some unknown guy delivered it to our security and told them to hand this over to you. As I was completely submerged in despair and agony, I threw that gift box to the ground. This impact caused that box to break open, and a letter and a crystal Bluebird with its wings wide open, slid out of it. Stunned and confused, I picked that crystal bluebird in one hand and the letter in the other, and saw who wrote it to me. It was from Cherry. With great excitement, I started reading it....

Letter

I hated myself. I hated myself for loving you. If you hadn't been with me that day, I could have somehow saved granny. Not a day goes by, when I don't blame us for the incident. I know it has affected you too. When you asked me for redemption, I was already numb. I couldn't figure out the trauma. I just had to leave the place to move on. When I left Norway, I was convinced that was the end of us. But you proved me wrong. When I tried to get you out from the island, you always feared to step out. But now, you showed me that the strength of your desire to meet me is stronger than your worst fears. If I don't recognize your efforts now, there's no point in all my yearning in the past for you to come out. Yes Joe, what you said on that live stream while announcing the concert was absolutely true. All my disgust is only over your fears and disabilities, but not over you. Thanks for making me to realize this. If you ditch your fears, there will be nothing to hate about you.

Everyone was considering you as a failure in the concert. But I can see the good happening in you. With all my perished hopes came alive, I want you to hear this from me. Hear this for the only time that I'm saying it, this will be your only way to redemption. I'm starting to accept you but not with your fears. I would like to meet you, not as Joe whom I knew, but as Joseph Edward Bell, a wholly new person who had quit his fears for good. You are already on your way. Keep on. Walk over your fears, face them in full vigour and fight them. It is not easy to travel from the north pole to the equator, from solitude to union. It is not easy to carry your fears across the oceans and still explore new lands. I know this because I know you. I also know what you're trying to prove. By flying down to Agra, you've shown the desire to find me. With the concert, you've shown what you are willing to sacrifice for me. I saw you on stage. I saw you fight your fears and still hold hope. I must say, I'm impressed. For this, I really want to share the most important news with you. 3 days back, on my work trip to Thenzawl, a town in the state called Mizoram, I discovered Diamond of kinabalu orchid plants with fully bloomed flowers in the nursery garden named Green-treasures. I know that by knowing this information you will be avid to paint your precious memory. But Joe, you cannot fill the canvas with joyful emotion without pursuing the happiness around. I have said this to you many times in the past but you have not tried to do so.

I want you to go to Thenzawl and get the plant yourself. With all my longing for you to successfully paint your memory, here is a little gift of crystal Bluebird in flying pose. This gift is not just as any other gift, I hope you can decode and understand my intent through it.
Until next time,
Cherry....

After reading the letter and finding words of encouragement from Cherry, I collapsed in the middle of the room with joy and screamed out in a merry mood.

Initially I couldn't understand why Cherry wanted me to go and get the plant by myself? I just felt that she wanted me to face this world, so that I could get some courage to cope with my fears. I know going to Thenzawl was going to be a battle within me, which I have to win definitely to prove my change to Cherry. Being aware that this was the final chance from Cherry to trust my change, I headed to Thenzawl. But alongside coping with my fears there was another significant reason behind making me to step out for that plant which I have perceived lately. . . 'Bluebird is a symbolism of happiness. Sending this bird in flying pose, Cherry intended me to fly out from my confinement to chase happiness'. . . By making me step out in the name of getting that plant, Cherry made me chase happiness. This not only helped me to depict true joy in my painting, but also made me derive happiness in my life.

When I surrendered to my fears and gave up hope, Cherry refused, stood behind, left off all her desires, went through a lot of suffering and terrible losses but eventually scripted a great turnaround in my life. As a gratitude for making me find the lost happiness in my life, I honoured Cherry by releasing the song as per her desire.

My agonized life ended when dad put me out of death. Since then, it's been a whole new life for me. My journey from the far ends of the north pole to the cramped streets of India, made me find the real meaning of life. I could now see a better connection between things despite my fears still lurking inside me.

AS A MEMORY OF OUR LOVE

Next day.... Early in the morning, I made my way to Mehtab Bagh (which was a garden aligned with the Taj Mahal on the opposite bank). I went there to plant a rose sapling as a memory of our love, same as Cherry had done in the past. Though I didn't meet Cherry after reaching Agra, I felt that planting a plant near to the Taj Mahal would represent my love for Cherry and my good times in this country.

When I was planting that rose sapling, as there was no beard and wig covering my face now, people who were present there recognized me and started papping me. Some of them had even tried to approach me for selfies. But my security officials stopped them from reaching me. Watching that group of people, I started to get nervous. My heartbeat raised, my hands trembled, and sweat began to ooze out from my skin. In this edgy state, I quickly completed to plant with my shivering hands. Then I walked away from them.... After putting a few steps forward, I suddenly stopped. I stopped because I didn't want my fears to pull me down anymore. So fighting against my fears, I decided to face the group and turned at them by wiping out my sweat. I then gestured to my security to allow them. With the permission granted, those people approached me with great excitement and asked for selfies. Though I was extremely nervous, I agreed to their request and posed for selfies with them with an uncomfortable smile.

CHERRY:

FULFILLMENT

Knowing that Joe was in Methab Bagh, I reached there and kept watching him from a distance. Joe's interaction with those people brought a great delight in me. I was glad to see Joe stepping out from his confinement. At the time when all my hopes perished, Joe arrived here crossing all his barriers. Though I was completely enraged at Joe's approach initially, his vigorous efforts to reach me by battling against his fears mollified my rage. I have been tailing Joe since he announced his concert. I have even tailed him at Thenzawl, when I visited there on my regular botanical work trips for Senna who was my client. Through Senna, I came to know that Joe was staying in his farmhouse. When I went there, I saw Joe relishing with kids. I saw Joe battling his fears to conquer the darkness around him to find the beauty of his life in the light. Joe's bold decision to stay at Thenzawl impressed me a lot. I didn't think that he will stay back there when I asked him to go to Thenzawl. When I constantly tried to bring Joe out from his confinement in the past, I never succeeded. I even formulated a plan with Aston to make Joe step out of his captivity. After a great deal of effort, Aston and I came to know that we could possibly find Diamond of Kinabalu orchid plant at Myrdal and Vossevangen. Believing that Joe could witness the beauty of this world and happiness around, I took him there in the name of getting that plant. But as usual, he didn't show any interest in my efforts other than getting the plant. Despite these previous futile efforts,

Joe's successful completion of painting by questing his joy in Thenzawl, eventually made me happy. I have to agree that he kept on impressing me. The pain and agony induced by Joe, was now pacified by witnessing him thrive.

My absence made Joe battle over his fears, I believe my absence will make him more persistent to reach me by conquering his fears. If I forgive him now, he may stop in his progress. Walking over his fears is the only way left for Joe to flourish. I hope this makes him progress as a person. Until Joe's fears are completely dispelled, I cannot forgive him. Until this happens, I will guide him from behind. His change is the biggest tribute which Joe can pay to granny. Till I find a new Joseph Edward Bell, I will keep on searching for him inside Joe.

~

Note: 'Diamond of Kinabalu orchid' is a fictional plant. But there is a similar kind of plant called 'Gold of Kinabalu orchid'. Many traits of this fictional plant were taken from Gold of Kinabalu orchid. As 'Gold of Kinabalu orchid' flowers doesn't have fragrance, and other rare plants do not match the requirements of the story and setting, I decided to go with a fictional plant.

Disclaimer: The use of medicine names in the book is for fictional purpose only and is not intended to endorse or promote them.

CREDITS:

Editor & adviser: Rohit D.

Contributors: Anurag B.   Sumanth D.   Sri Girinath P.
Ganesh B.

Help in regard to medical research: Dr Sandeep.   Dr Harish
Laxman.   Dr Cyril.

My sincere thanks to everyone who contributed to the book.
Kumar,
Author.

****

9 798887 335155